The sky, as perfectly clear as it had been the day before, was beginning to show signs of light when Orl brought the car to a stop in what appeared to be a dry creek bed. A hill, covered with the same white-trunked, large-leaved trees that had been around the Earth Gate, was on their right, away from the rising sun.

"The Temple city is over that hill," Orl said, pointing. The side panels of their car vanished and them climbed out.

"Kari and I have scouted this place before," Orl explained. "I can point out to you the building I believe to be the Temple. Kari and I will remain here until you return."

"And if I don't return?" Ross inquired.

"Then Kari and I will decide what to do next."

It wasn't, Ross thought, all that comforting a reply. Kari, who had started to lead the way up the hill, turned and grinned at him, and Ross rather surprisingly found himself reassured. Warrior societies, he recalled, generally placed great emphasis on aiding one's comrades. He tramped up the hill after her, with Orl in the rear, making more noise than both the humans combined. Kari was as silent as a ghost, and Ross had been on enough hunting trips to be a moderately good woodsman, but Orl was definitely a city type. When they were within a few yards of the top, Kari motioned Ross and Orl to stop while she crouched down and eased herself slowly to the crest. A moment later, Ross heard her sharp intake of breath, and he tensed half expecti... dozen black-clad barba... over the hill afte...

THE FIRST TWELVE
LASER BOOKS

\# 1 .... **Renegades of Time**
by Raymond F. Jones

\# 2 .... **Herds**
by Stephen Goldin

\# 3 .... **Crash Landing On Iduna**
by Arthur Tofte

\# 4 .... **Gates of the Universe**
by R. Coulson and G. DeWeese

\# 5 .... **Walls Within Walls**
by Arthur Tofte

\# 6 .... **Serving in Time**
by Gordon Eklund

\# 7 .... **Seeklight**
by K. W. Jeter

\# 8 .... **Caravan**
by Stephen Goldin

\# 9 .... **Invasion**
by Aaron Wolfe

\#10 .... **Falling Toward Forever**
by Gordon Eklund

\#11 .... **Unto The Last Generation**
by Juanita Coulson

\#12 .... **The King of Eolim**
by Raymond F. Jones

ROBERT COULSON AND GENE DEWEESE

GATES OF THE UNIVERSE

Cover
Illustration by
KELLY FREAS

GATES OF THE UNIVERSE

A LASER BOOK / first published 1975

© 1975 by Robert Coulson and Gene DeWeese

ISBN 0-373-72004-1

LASER BOOKS are published by Harlequin Enterprises
Limited, 240 Duncan Mill Road, Don Mills, Ontario M3B 1Z4,
Canada. The Laser Books trade mark, consisting of the words
"LASER BOOKS" is registered in the Canada Trade Marks
Office, the United States Patent Office, and in other
countries.

Printed in U.S.A.

CHAPTER 1

Ross Allen lowered the bulldozer blade and began another pass at the diminishing hillside. Another half day, he thought, and we'll have it licked. Provided, of course, that we don't run into any more boulders like the one last week. Hitting a ton of firmly embedded rock unexpectedly does nothing at all for the effectiveness of a bulldozer blade. But it wasn't likely that he would run into two rocks that size on one job, and besides, the chewing out he'd received from construction boss Joe Kujawa had speeded up his reflexes considerably.

Fastest shift in the midwest, he mused a trifle smugly as he tilted the blade to match the changing contour of the hill.

A screech like a million pieces of chalk on a giant blackboard—or a bulldozer blade on a large rock—split the air and set Ross's teeth painfully on edge. The ear-piercing shriek stopped a fraction of a second later as Ross's hands flew over the controls; the blade lifted and the treads stopped.

After giving his ears and teeth a moment to recover, Ross stood up and peered over the blade as best he could. All he could see was that the pile of dirt he had been shoving had tumbled back and covered whatever the blade had grated against. He glanced over his shoulder and saw that Kujawa, who had been supervising the compacting machines a hundred yards away, had heard the screech and was galloping to investigate.

Ross locked the brakes and climbed down over one of the treads. He was squatting in front of the blade, tossing lumps of dirt aside, when Kujawa came pounding up. After a quick inspection of the blade, the construction boss turned on Ross.

Ross sighed inwardly. As usual during his conversations with Ross, Joe Kujawa's craggy face was twisted into a scowl, making him look even meaner than the broken nose and malformed jaw—the results of a long-ago accident—made him look normally. Joe was actually a couple of inches shorter than Ross, but somehow his stocky body always seemed to loom over Ross's six-foot height. With his hard hat pushed to the back of his wiry greying hair, he looked like a cross between a cigarette ad and the villain of a TV detective show.

"Okay, let's see what you managed to ram into this time," Kujawa growled as he looked past Ross at the small patch of rock that Ross had uncovered.

"It's flat," Ross said, frowning as he poked at the area with his finger. "And smooth. Really smooth, like glass."

"So? You never seen a flat rock before? Lucky for you it was flat; if it had been an ordinary old rock like the one you creamed into last week, you'd be in trouble. You're just lucky, you know it? Well, don't just sit there with your mouth open; you're not catching flies. Get that thing scraped off. I'll go get some dynamite, just in case; we ain't got time to fool around."

Kujawa straightened up and started back across the muddy field.

"Wait a minute!" Ross yelled over the rumble of the idling bulldozer motor. "This isn't just a rock! It's too smooth; it feels like a finished surface of some kind."

The construction boss swung around irritably. One

hand jerked the yellow hard hat off while the other ran through his hair, leaving it with the appearance of a grey haystack.

"Big deal!" he roared. "So it's smooth; so you polished it some with the blade! Fifteen feet below the surface makes it a rock. I suppose you think you struck one of them archeo-whatchacallits in the middle of Indiana? Or do you think it's a petrified flying saucer? Get it outta there!"

"But . . ." Ross began.

"And another thing," Kujawa non-sequitered, "tell that pal of yours to quit calling you at work. I got enough problems without taking your phone calls; I ain't your secretary."

Ross looked totally blank for a moment while his mind strove to follow the abrupt change of subject. Then a grin started across his features as he realized who the caller must have been, and was hastily suppressed before Kujawa could ask him what he was laughing at.

"You mean Roehm?" he shouted after Kujawa, who was spun about and was slogging purposefully away.

"Yeah, that's the one," Kujawa shouted back over his shoulder. "If you get that rock cleared out of there by the time I get back, I might tell you what he said."

Ross watched Kujawa's retreating back for several seconds, feeling his stomach beginning to twitch expectantly. It was probably premature, but Ed Roehm knew better than to call Ross on the job unless it was for something pretty important. Maybe the little literary agent had finally found a publisher for Ross's projected adventures series. That would be great; if *Commander Freff, Interstellar Agent* had been sold, even if it was only the first three, then Ross could afford to quit driving a bulldozer and begin full-time writing. In fact, he would have to. The one contract he already had was due in a couple of months, and if the Freff series was sold. . . .

With an effort, Ross pulled himself back to earth. He had no real idea why Roehm had called. Maybe it wasn't a sale. Maybe, he thought suddenly, the little coward was throwing in the towel! Maybe. . . .

Well, he'd better not risk antagonizing Kujawa any more than his mere presence seemed to do, at least until he found out for sure what was going on.

Five minutes later, Ross sat on the bulldozer's seat, staring in fascination at the area he had uncovered. It was, he decided, highly unlikely if not totally impossible. He had seen slabs of natural rock before, and they just did not come like this. There were no such things in nature as perfectly flat, glassy, twenty-foot squares of rock. This was the sort of nonsense that Commander Freff was likely to run into, not a reasonably sane and respectable Ross Allen.

Ross shook his head. *Come on,* he thought. *You're letting your imagination take over again. This is just a big, flat, glassy rock. Obsidian, maybe; or is it some other kind of rock that's flat and glassy? Anyway, what else could it be? Flat smooth rocks are much more likely than. . . .*

Than what?

Not knowing what else it might be, Ross decided to tackle it from another angle. Obviously, if it had been discovered by Commander Freff instead of Ross Allen, it would be a diabolical machine of some kind. That was the way the Commander's adventures operated. A diabolical machine here, a sinister nemesis there; it all added up. This would undoubtedly be something left

8

behind by the Naissur Empire when the Naissur had retreated from this sector of space a hundred centuries before. Now, then, exactly what would this diabolical alien machine do?

Plotting happily, Ross raised the bulldozer blade and absently started forward. Better make one last pass to clear off the far corner of the square and then get the machine out of the way before Kujawa arrived with the dynamite. This thing wasn't going to be shoved out of the way by any mere bulldozer.

While Ross started the machine across the rock, most of his mind was intent on Commander Freff, who continued to examine the enigmatic surface in an effort to enucleate the kernel of its awesome potentiality.

I wonder if that's a bit much for the readers? Ross thought. *Oh well, science fiction is supposed to be educational; let them look up the hard words. Now, where was I?*

Commander Freff leaned down, his nose almost touching the slab, and peered closely at the milky surface. Was that a faint swirling motion he descried in the depths? What did it all mean? This primitive planet was at the very fringe of galactic civilization; could the ancient Naissur have penetrated this far? Their home world was. . . .

Commander Freff and his speculations vanished abruptly as a cold wind suddenly struck Ross in the face and he was plunged into sudden and total darkness. At the same instant, his ears popped, as though he had just shot down several floors in a fast elevator. For a moment he froze, but his reflexes took over and quickly threw the transmission into neutral and locked the brakes.

9

I've gone blind! he thought. *"But why? What happened? I wasn't doing anything!*

He blinked strenuously, rolled his eyes, and finally twisted around on the seat and peered into the blackness all around him in a vain attempt to see something—anything. His right hand still clutched the gear shift and the bulldozer's powerful diesel engine rumbled and shook, informing him that he was still on the machine, but his vision provided no information at all. He brought his left hand up to rub at his eyes—and heaved a sigh of relief.

He wasn't blind, after all! The luminous dial of his watch glowed at him comfortingly.

But if he wasn't blind, then what was he? *Where* was he?

A few seconds ago he had been in the middle of a ten-acre construction site, in broad daylight. But if nothing had happened to his eyes, then had suddenly something happened to the sun? Or was he now in a different location? Now that the initial horror of possible blindness had been removed, he felt almost calm. Certainly calm enough to think and observe; but what was there to observe, aside from the dial of his watch?

Sounds? He brought the watch to his ear, verifying that it was still running, and that very little time had elapsed since he last checked it. The only other sound was the rumble of the bulldozer as it idled, the loud, echoing rumble of. . . .

Echoing? It not only echoed, but reverberated. Which meant that he was now inside of something? Some kind of cave? The slab had been the roof of a huge cavern of some kind, and the bulldozer had fallen through? But then why hadn't both he and the bulldozer been smashed

10

to bits? A bulldozer produces disastrous effects if it falls very far.

Ross looked upward hopefully, but the blackness overhead was just as thick as it was everywhere else. No open hole above him that he had fallen through, then.

What else? A land mine of some kind? The slab had exploded when the bulldozer had driven over it, and he had been killed instantly? But that would mean that the bulldozer had died, too, and gone with him to wherever he was. Scratch that theory.

Amnesia? He had blacked out mentally and driven the bulldozer some place where he could black out physically? *That's a ridiculous idea even for your imagination,* he told himself sternly. *Besides, no time has passed.*

And there was the wind, a soft wind blowing lightly on him from all directions. What could be causing that?

Something thumped against the back of the bulldozer. Ross jerked around in the seat as a familiar voice crackled up out of the darkness.

"What's going on around here?" It was Joe Kujawa, and he sounded very irritated, even for Joe.

"Joe?" Ross's voice barely carried over the sound of the diesel.

"That you, Allen? What dumb stunt have you pulled now?" The irritation was giving way to panic around the edges. The voice was a full octave higher at the end of the question.

Ross throttled down the engine and the resulting alteration of sound brought another outburst from Kujawa.

"Dammit, Allen, say something! Is that you or not, you clown? And if it is you, why don't you turn on your lights?"

11

Lights!

So much for the calm and rational Ross Allen. How long had he been sitting here, wondering where he was, while the switch to turn on all four lamps had been only inches from his hands? He reached for the switch, wondering if perhaps his subconscious had *wanted* to stay in the dark. He blinked as the lamps on the four corners of the machine flared to life.

A huge, windowless, doorless room stretched around him. It was at least twenty feet high and fifty yards across. The floor was bare, and the forward lights shone directly on a gigantic mural that completely covered one wall. It was a magnificent view of a lush, green valley, but with something oddly wrong about the foliage, something that Ross couldn't quite place. On the far side of the valley, a brilliantly colored needle of a building towered elegantly above the surrounding greenery. Across the top of the mural, near the twenty-foot high ceiling, was a slogan: "During your stopover, visit the Tower Restaurant."

Looking around, Ross saw Kujawa standing just behind the bulldozer. His mouth was slightly ajar and he was clutching a dozen or so sticks of dynamite in both hands. He was staring blankly at another billboard-like mural, this one featuring a harsh sun beating down on endless vista of sand, grotesque lava flows, a few scraggly bushes, and several unpleasantly reptilian animals. Letters across a cloudless, not-quite-blue sky announced: "Something different for the hardy traveler."

"Joe?" Ross spoke weakly.

At the sound of the voice, Kujawa's jaw snapped shut and he spun around, squinting into the glare of the lights.

"Ross, you idiot!" he exploded. "Nobody else would

be fool enough to sit here with the lights off for half an hour. Well, you really did it this time. How did you manage to get us in *here?*"

Ross's calm, which had totally deserted him at the sight of the huge room and the murals, was partly restored by Kujawa's familiar voice. It was exactly the same as it had sounded for weeks at the construction site; even in the open air that bull roar had seemed to echo a bit.

"More to the point," he answered, "would be to find out where 'here' is."

"What? Whaddaya mean? You got us here! If you don't know where we are, who does?"

"I got *us* here?" Ross replied, aggrieved. "I suppose I must have got myself here, though I don't know how. But as for you. . . ."

"Yes, you got us here. You and your dozer just disappeared into thin air. Naturally, I run over to see what happened, and. . . ."

"Disappeared? Literally?"

"Yeah, disappeared. Literally or any other way you want to call it." Kujawa gestured with the dynamite in what Ross considered a reckless manner. "I run over to see where you'd got to, and all of a sudden everything goes black and I fetch up against the back of the dozer."

The glimmer of an idea entered Ross's mind, and was rejected instantly. To a science fiction writer it was an obvious answer, but not one that he wanted to believe could happen to him. To Commander Freff, maybe, but not to Ross Allen. Obviously he had disappeared from the construction site, and obviously he had appeared here, wherever "here" was. Thus the slab had to be some kind of transportation device, and it had transported Ross, the bulldozer, and Kujawa

13

somewhere. Or perhaps somewhen. Unfortunately, this explanation was utterly impossible and ridiculous. There must be a rational, logical explanation somewhere. But what could it be?

Ross shook his head. What he needed now was some of Commander Freff's amazing but fictional acumen. If the Commander got involved in something like this, what would he do?

"The Commander!" Ross exclaimed aloud, suddenly recalling that when last sighted, the Commander had been busily examining the slab. Of course. He leaped down from the bulldozer, dropped to his knees and began examining the floor, while Kujawa watched with the gloomy expression of someone who has just watched a friend carted off to a home for the mentally bewildered. Ignoring the construction boss, Ross ran his hands over the floor, almost immediately discovering a hairline crack running parallel to the bulldozer tread. A few feet behind the machine, the crack, almost imperceptible to the eye, intersected a second crack perpendicular to the first. Following the cracks with his fingers, Ross traced a large square on the floor of the building. He couldn't be positive, but it looked to be of identical size and material to the original slab back on the construction site.

So the Commander—and Ross's sudden intuition—had been right after all! Impossible as it seemed, that innocent-appearing slab had been a matter transmitter of some kind. It was the only possible way of getting from *there* to *here* with no loss of time in the transition.

"I told you that rock was too smooth to be natural," Ross said.

"Rock? What's a rock got to do with. . . ."

"It was a machine!" Ross explained. "Probably a

matter transmitter. Or I suppose it could have been a time machine. Anyway, it acted like a sort of gate between the construction site and wherever we are now. Or whenever."

It was amazing, he thought, how the words rolled off his tongue, as if he actually knew what they meant. It gave him the same sense of euphoria he had felt a few years ago, when he had watched two men hopping around on the Moon. Until that moment, space travel had never seemed quite real; it was something to read about. But that night he had watched it all happening.

Now he was calmly explaining to his boss that they had just gone through a matter transmitter. He had never really believed in matter transmitters before, even while he was writing about them. Now they had become real.

Or at least, they had become real to him. Kujawa was still having a little trouble. "If this is some kind of joke. . . ." he began.

"No joke," Ross reassured him. "Or if it is, it's on both of us." Ross privately complimented himself on that line. The Commander himself couldn't have done better.

"I haven't the faintest idea where we are, but I think the main problem is to get back," he continued.

"Sure," Kujawa said. "We're already behind schedule, mainly because you like to hit rocks. Okay; you got us here, you get us out. I keep telling you that, and you keep sitting there like a dummy."

"Couldn't we look around a little, first?" Ross said. "After all, we're the first people to set foot on this world." (*Then who built the transmitter?* said a nagging little voice inside his head. Ross told it to shut up.) "What fun would it have been to watch the Moon land-

15

ing if the astronauts had jumped out of the rocket, said a few words, and then turned around and left right away?"

"Them astronauts didn't have no building site to get leveled off by next Friday," Joe said. "You ain't doing no joy-riding on a company bulldozer, so just get us back where we come from."

Ross thought resentfully that people like Kujawa had probably told Columbus to forget the whole thing because they were behind schedule at the shipyard. But Kujawa was the boss, so Ross reluctantly climbed back on the bulldozer.

"As I see it," he said, "this slab we're on got us here, so probably it can take us back. Driving the bulldozer over it must have triggered it somehow, so driving over it again should get us back. Climb on and we'll get started."

"Now you're talking," Kujawa said. "Here, take some of these so I can have a hand free." He casually tossed most of the dynamite, with caps and fuses already attached, up to Ross, who clutched them frantically. Stuffing the rest of the explosive casually into his belt, Kujawa clambered up over the tread and stood on the fender back of the massive tool box. Ross stowed his share of the dynamite more cautiously, unlocked the brakes, put the bulldozer in gear, and backed across the square.

Nothing happened.

"Well?" Kujawa's voice was loud in his ear.

Ross shifted to forward and the machine clanked across the square again. The soft wind still blew. They were still inside the huge building.

Braking the left tread, Ross swung the dozer around

16

and tried again. There was only the wind as they drove across.

He was maneuvering to come at the square from another side when he heard a voice. It was faint over the roar of the diesel, and he shifted to neutral.

The voice was coming from the square.

Ross set the brakes and jumped down, with Kujawa following him dubiously. The wind felt stranger to Ross as he stood directly in the center of the square, straining his ears.

The voice came sharp and clear. "Where could they go, anyway? Joe said he was going to get this thing dynamited."

"That's Sam!" Ross exclaimed, recognizing the voice of Sam Southworth, the other bulldozer operator. "Sam, we're right here! Can't you hear me?"

Apparently Sam couldn't. His voice continued, presumably aimed at someone standing some distance away. Then another, softer voice answered, gradually becoming louder as its owner approached what Ross was beginning to think of as "The Gate". The new voice was also familiar, and finally Ross identified it as that of Hal Sanders, the construction company owner.

Kujawa recognized it at about the same time. "What's he doing out here?" he muttered resentfully. "Checking up on me, I bet. That. . . ."

"You don't know where old Joe went to, then?" The second voice came through again.

"Nossir. He went and got some dynamite from the shack a good ten minutes ago. Said Allen had rammed another rock. This one, I reckon."

"Yeah. Big old thing. Wonder how it got that polish on it? I surely do hope it's not going to hold us up.

17

Sam, you better go pick up some more dynamite. If you see old Joe, tell him I want to talk to him, but don't waste any time looking for him. Better pick up a drill, too. We'll want one charge right in the middle of it, to break it up. Ask Jaeger if he's seen that other bulldozer, too."

"Okay. Last time I saw it, Allen had it. It was right over here someplace. You know, that's kind of funny. Like I was just saying to Rivera last night. . . ."

"Yeah, yeah. Well, two men and a bulldozer can't just vanish off the face of the earth. They'll turn up. And when they do," Sanders' voice took on a grim note, "I want to see them!"

As the voices began to fade, the euphoria which had been sustaining Ross suddenly vanished. This wasn't just watching a couple of trained astronauts on tv; this was happening to *him*. Those voices, coming from out of thin air, were coming from Earth. From an Earth that they would never be able to return to unless they did something fast.

"Hal!" he yelled frantically, "we're right here! Don't blow that rock!" Kujawa joined him in shouting. There was no reply; no indication that they could be heard.

After a minute or so the futility of yelling dawned on Ross; the bulldozer could make more racket than he and Kujawa combined, and if nobody had heard that. . . . Anyway, his throat was getting sore.

"Whatever it is," he said, "it looks like it only works one way. All we can do is hope that somebody comes through while somebody else is watching. If they blow that rock before we figure out how to reverse it, we'll never get back."

Kujawa was looking rather nervously around the huge room. "I think maybe you got something there," he said. "If this thing's a machine like you said, it's got to have a set of controls somewhere. Stands to reason. All we got to do is find them."

"Don't bet on it," Ross said, but he began looking at the surrounding area anyway. It gave him something to do besides think about what would happen if Sanders blew up that rock.

The floor, he saw, was perfectly smooth except for the square in the center. Something odd about that; the dividing line had been all but invisible earlier, but now it was plainly marked. The entire floor looked like grey marble, dusty but totally unmarked. Even the bulldozer treads had only made trails in the dust; they had not scratched that floor. Each wall was devoted to a huge mural. The views had a startlingly three-dimensional effect, and he wondered briefly why he hadn't noticed that before. Too confused by the strange surroundings, maybe. Each mural showed a magnificent but somewhat alien landscape, with what was apparently an advertisement printed across the top. And wonder of wonders, Ross thought, the messages were all in English. Which meant. . . .

He blinked and looked at the messages again, and abruptly felt numb. Shock, he told himself. He was going into shock.

"Joe," he said after a few seconds of staring at the messages, "can you read that writing on the wall?"

"Sure I can," Kujawa said without pausing in his inspection of a small shelf in a corner of the room. "It ain't just you college kids know how to read. They ain't control labels, so quit sightseeing on company time and look for something useful."

"What language are they in?" Ross persisted.

"English, of course! What do they look like?"

"Like nothing I've ever seen before. Take another look, Joe. A good one."

Kujawa snorted derisively, but turned to look at the desert scene. "Just a bunch of ads," he muttered. "Like that one, for. . . ." His voice trailed off and he blinked and squinted at the characters. His eyes darted at Ross for a moment, then went to a second wall.

"But it's got to be English!" he insisted. "It's the only language I know!"

Oddly, Ross felt relief, now that he was sure that he and Kujawa were seeing the same thing. He wasn't insane after all, or if he was, he wasn't alone.

"Obviously it isn't English," he said. "And equally obviously, we can both read it."

"What's the difference?" Kujawa retorted suddenly, a shutter clicking down in his mind. "All it means is that we can read the control directions when we find them."

He was right, of course, Ross realized. Even standing around talking about it was simply wasting time; time that they didn't have to waste. Hurriedly, he followed Kujawa's lead and began moving around the walls, examining every minor irregularity that might indicate a control panel or a doorway to a separate control room. But even as he searched, a detached part of his mind continued to occupy itself with other things, such as Commander Freff.

If only he had a camera! Nobody was ever going to believe this. He probably wouldn't believe it himself, once he got back home. Besides, there were times when Commander Freff could use an authentic looking alien language, and the insane hieroglyphics on the walls would be perfect, if he could find a publisher willing to set them in type. In fact, this whole episode would make a good beginning for one of the Commander's adventures.

If he ever got back home to write it.

By now, Ross and Kujawa had inspected, poked at, and felt all four walls and the floor and found nothing but a lot of dust and two completely barren shelves set into opposite corners. The only breaks in either walls or floor were the lines outlining the square in the center of the floor. Ross returned to the square, panic and frustration growing by the second. The wind still blew softly out of nowhere, and as he was about to start on a second useless search of the walls, a voice filtered through.

"It's about time!" It was Sanders again. "Here, give me that stuff."

Moments later, there were clanking sounds, and then the whine of an electric drill. Then Southworth, some distance away, announced that the detonator was ready. Ross felt as if the world was closing in on him, collapsing and suffocating him. They really were going to blow up that slab before he and Joe could get back.

"Hal!" Ross screamed. "You blow that thing up and you'll never get your bulldozer back!"

There was no reaction, except that Kujawa abandoned his disconsolate inspection of a wall and ran toward the bulldozer.

"It's got to be the bulldozer!" Ross said. "It's our only chance; somehow that's got to be the key." He leaped for the machine as he spoke, with Kujawa following. Ross climbed into the seat and put the machine into gear as Kujawa clambered aboard behind him, gripping the back of the seat.

"Think about Earth!" Ross yelled over the roar of the machine. "Maybe it works on telepathy. I was thinking about an alien planet when I drove over it the first time."

"I wasn't!" Kujawa snapped, but he gritted his teeth and appeared to be concentrating.

Ross did his best to banish all thoughts of the Commander and visualise the vast muddy construction site as he had last seen it. There were the remains of the hill he had been cutting away, the already flattened areas were the compacting machines had been working, the trees a hundred yards away to the west, and the busy highway an equal distance to the east. The blue, almost cloudless sky. . . .

The bulldozer nosed into the square. The wind hit them, and Sanders' voice drifted through. Nothing else happened.

Leaving the machine in high gear, Ross put the brakes to one tread as soon as they cleared the square. Kujawa tightened his grip on the seat as the machine spun like a mammoth top and started back over the square again. Ross shifted down to first gear, and they moved with agonizing slowness. Nothing. There was only the wind, and the ominous sound of a drill. They must be nearly ready to place the charge by now, Ross thought frantically. Why couldn't just one of them walk through? Why hadn't the transmitter worked when Sanders walked out on the slab to start drilling?

He threw the bulldozer back into high gear and spun it again. This time he crossed the square from corner to corner. Nothing. Off the other side, another spin, another pass. He lowered the blade until it screamed as it scraped across the floor. A different angle, a different speed. Nothing happened.

"They'll touch it off any second now," Kujawa bellowed in his ear. "And if we're right on top of it. . . ."

Ross hesitated for only a moment. Whatever the effect was, it appeared to be one-way. If energy in the form of sound waves came through, it was logical that energy in the form of exploding dynamite would come through, too. Already headed across the square, Ross kept going, lifted the blade, and headed for the wall ahead, wishing it was farther away from the center of the building.

They were within a few feet of the wall when a large section of it vanished, revealing a sunlit ramp that led upward. Ross gunned the machine through the opening, and suddenly there was a roar behind them, and a million fists hit his unprotected shoulders and head. Kujawa, exposed to the full force of the blast, was blown completely off the bulldozer. Even as Ross applied the brakes, he noticed that both the noise and the force of the explosion had cut off sharply.

As the bulldozer ground to a halt, Ross turned to look back into the room. The back end of the machine almost filled the doorway, but he could see that while the square seemed unmarked, there were chunks of dirt scattered around, and mixed with them were pieces of what looked suspiciously like parts of the original slab from the construction site.

Ross leaped down from the machine and dashed back to the square, ignoring Kujawa, who was shaking his head and struggling to his feet. The sudden cessation of the explosion filled his mind as he ran. He was sure of what he would find at the square, but he had to confirm it.

He stopped at the center of the square, listening. There were no sounds, no voices; only the noise of the bulldozer idling. The soft breeze from nowhere had stopped.

The Gate, whatever it had been, was closed.

23

CHAPTER 2

Ross stood in the center of the square, without thinking, almost without feeling. The sound of the explosion played itself back in his mind again and again, as if its overwhelming roar, repeated over and over, could drown out the silence that hovered over him now; the silence that meant that as far as he and Kujawa were concerned, Earth no longer existed.

After a long time there amid the scattered chunks of dirt and rock that were his last links with Earth, he began to start thinking again. After all, if anyone was ever prepared to handle something like this, he was. He'd dumped his heroes in situations like this often enough, and they all survived.

They, however, were heroes, not real people. Each one had more muscle and knowledge than he and Kujawa combined, and in addition they always had him to look out for them and dig them out of any holes they got into. A wave of despair swept over Ross as he looked again at the chunks of Earth scattered about.

"What happened?"

It was Kujawa. Ross blinked and looked around. The construction boss was leaning unsteadily against one tread of the bulldozer.

"Just what we expected," Ross said as he walked toward Kujawa. "They blew it up." He leaned down and picked up a hunk of dirt. It crumbled in his hands, and the bits fell to the floor.

"Blew it up?" Kujawa seemed dazed.

Ross nodded. "We're on our own now. Even if we found some controls, there's nothing left to control with them."

Kujawa was still staring blankly as Ross reached the bulldozer and started to climb onto the machine. Suddenly the older man's face twisted into a mask of anger, and he lunged at Ross, his heavy, muscular arms reaching out.

"You son of a bitch!" he shouted, grabbing Ross's shirt. "You did this! You got us stuck here!"

Caught off balance, Ross flailed his arms as he was yanked from his position on the tread of the bulldozer. Somehow, he came down on his feet, reeling backward. His shirt tore loose from Kujawa's grip as he stumbled away.

"Joe, come on. What's got into you?"

Kujawa wasn't listening. He advanced on Ross, his face still twisted in anger. Ross began to wonder if the combined physical and mental shocks had been too much for the construction boss; the man acted as if he had suddenly gone insane. You were supposed to be gentle with the mentally afflicted, Ross remembered, and humor them—if they'd let you.

"Look, Joe, whoever was at fault we're in this together. Can't you. . . ?"

Joe couldn't. He leaped forward and Ross retreated, only to find that he was trapped. There wasn't room for him to get between the sidewall of the ramp and the tread of the bulldozer, and Joe wasn't going to give him time to climb over the machine. Ross's eyes darted around, looking for something he could use to defend himself. He was younger than Kujawa, but the construction boss was a veteran of a hundred rough-and-tumble battles and Ross knew that in a bare-handed fight he wouldn't have a chance. It looked as though bare hands were all he had, though.

Then, as Kujawa advanced again, Ross felt something poke at his stomach; the dynamite sticks. Without thinking, he grabbed one of them, holding it up like a club. He started to swing it, aiming at Kujawa's head.

Abruptly, Kujawa's face returned to normal and he retreated out of range of Ross's swing. As Ross watched him tensely, he stared at Ross as though he had never seen him before, then he relaxed and chuckled.

Ross was shaking with reaction, but suddenly the ridiculousness of the situation struck him and he joined Kujawa in laughter. The construction boss was leaning against the bulldozer tread to prop himself up while the laughter shook his whole body. Finally it subsided enough for him to speak.

"Do you know how silly you looked, trying to brain me with that stick of dynamite?"

Ross grinned. "Well, I couldn't think of anything else. I thought you'd gone crazy."

Kujawa nodded. "Maybe I did, for a minute there. I don't know what came over me. I been in lots of fights, and some were pretty nasty. I bit half a man's ear off once," he said reflectively. "But I was always out to teach some punk a lesson, or give a good account of myself. That was the first time I've ever been really crazy mad at anyone. For a minute there I wanted to kill you. I never felt that way before, and there wasn't all that much reason for it this time. Even if you did get us into this mess."

"Well, let's hope you don't ever feel that way again, especially when I'm the only target. Since we aren't going to get back through the Gate, I suppose what we ought to do next is take a look around outside."

Kujawa nodded again. "Sure. Can't decide what we ought to do until we know where we are. Maybe there's another way to get home from here."

They turned to the bulldozer. "You really don't have any idea where this place is?" Kujawa asked.

Ross shook his head. "Not a one. If that thing really was a matter transmitter, we could be anywhere in the universe."

Saying the words helped Ross realize their implications, and he began to feel a sense of wonder. No matter what else happened to them, they had already become unique. Whatever that Gate was, they were the first people to go through it for thousands of years. Visions of mammoths and cave men and Inca pyramids and primitive men crossing Bering Strait flashed through his mind. He wondered which of the dozens of crackpot theories about "ancient astronauts" and prehistoric visitors from outer space came the closest to the truth. Maybe none of them. Just possibly he and Joe Kujawa were the first human beings to ever use this form of transportation; that Gate could have been put there by Arcturian arachnoids or some other of the bug-eyed monsters dear to science fiction writers, and never intended to have any connection with mankind.

By the time he and Kujawa had climbed onto the bulldozer and were ready to start off, the feeling of anticipation and curiosity that flooded through Ross totally overwhelmed any remnants of the despair that he had felt so strongly only minutes before. Here was an entire brand new world, probably never before seen by human eyes, and it was just waiting for him to look at it. He was, literally, living something out of one of his novels.

He put the bulldozer in gear and they started forward, up the ramp. As they moved out into the sunlight, he noted, with a faint twinge of disappointment, that the sky looked perfectly normal. A tint of green or orange overhead would have seemed more in keeping with an alien planet than this brilliant blue with a few greyish-white clouds scattered untidily about. The ramp made him think that the Gate in this world was located approximately the same distance underground as the stone slab had been on Earth. Had there once been a similar huge building among the prehistoric forests of Indiana?

Ross stopped the machine at the top of the ramp and looked around. The countryside seemed quite earthlike, although a heavy growth of vegetation prevented him from seeing much of it. The ramp emerged from the building and blended into a driveway of the same smooth material. As far as Ross could tell there was nothing actually growing through the pavement, but bushes leaned over it, and the growing branches and broken limbs of trees formed a tangle a few feet away. The greenery seemed quite like that around an abandoned farm on Earth. Ross could see nothing that seemed obviously alien or different, but then botany had never been one of his strong subjects.

And why, Ross thought suddenly, *am I assuming we're not on Earth? A time machine is just as likely as a matter transmitter is to another planet.*

Well, the only way to find out—if there was a way—was to look around, and they couldn't do much looking from here. Ross put the machine into gear, raised the blade as high as it would go to ward off the branches,

28

and plunged down the overgrown driveway at a thundering four miles per hour.

"Hang on, Joe," he said as the blade bit into the first tangle of branches, "we're off to see the Wizard."

Kujawa surprised Ross by saying, "If we fiind a hunk of tin with an axe in its hands, I'll know we've gone bananas. You know, I've seen that picture every year they had it on tv, I think. The kids loved it. I got so I sort of looked forward to it myself, they were so tickled. They . . ."

He broke off, the grin on his face faltering for a moment. "Come on," he said. "Won't this thing go any faster?"

For an instant, Ross saw images of his family and the girl he was going with, and, briefly this new world seemed dark and depressing. But with an effort, he shook off the mood. As the bulldozer continued to chew its way through the tangle of vegetation, he began looking at things more closely. A whole new world was here for examining.

Many of the trees were tropical looking. At least, they had large leaves like palms, but the bark corresponded more to Ross's vague recollections of birch. There were also many flowers, of the sort he usually associated with jungle movies, and he could hear creatures fluttering, chirping and complaining about the bulldozer's passage, though the animal life was keeping well out of sight. For a fraction of an instant he glanced toward the sun, as it popped briefly through the leaves overhead. It was hot and bright, and the blurred afterimage didn't seem noticeably different from the ones produced by Earth's sun. His knowledge, acquired for the Commander Freff series, that Sol was type G with a surface temperature of 6,000 degrees Kelvin didn't help much in identification. This sun wasn't a red giant or anything else exotic, but aside from that he couldn't tell anything.

Kujawa, who was fingering one of the broad leaves that he had snatched from one of the low hanging branches, suddenly looked up. "Did you hear something?" he asked.

Ross throttled down the diesel and listened. There was something; Kujawa must have good hearing. It was a hissing noise and was moving toward them and growing louder.

"Hang on again," Ross said as he shifted into a higher gear. "Maybe I can get us out where we can see what's going on."

The noise increased rapidly. Whatever was causing it went by only yards in front of them with a loud whoosh and the sound began diminishing rapidly. A few seconds later, the undergrowth disappeared and they saw that their driveway had led them to a paved road. The foliage was cleared back several yards from the road, and far to the left they could see something black and square disappearing into the distance. It looked as if it didn't quite touch the road's surface. Ross wondered if it might be a hovercraft, and resisted an impulse to try chasing it with the bulldozer.

An instant later, as Ross brought the bulldozer to a halt a few feet from the road, another of the black vehicles appeared around a bend in the road some distance to the right. As it swooped toward them, Ross had a moment to wonder if it wouldn't have been brighter to have stopped the bulldozer while it was still hidden from the road, and looked around a little on foot before barging out into a strange country. The thought of backing the machine up and shutting it off occurred to him, but only briefly. Turning off the huge diesel without letting it idle in neutral for several minutes was a good way to damage it, and damaging the bulldozer was one of the last things he wanted to do. Aside from being a last link with Earth, he just might need it in the near future.

By this time the alien car was only a few dozen yards away, still moving at the same speed as the first one. Then, abruptly, in a matter of only a few yards at most, it stopped. There was no squeal of brakes, no added roar of braking force, no sign of rocking or swaying. The vehicle simply stopped, about a hundred feet down the road from the watchers.

An instant later, most of the side of the car nearest Ross and Kujawa shimmered and disappeared. Someone, apparently the driver, leaped out of the car. The being appeared to be a normal human male, of indeterminate age. He was a couple of inches shorter than Ross's six-foot height, no brawnier than Ross's average physique, but with an air of strength about him. A vast quantity of beard, mustache, and bushy eyebrows concealed most of his face. He was dressed in what looked like a black uniform, and he was pulling something from his belt, for all the world like a traffic cop getting ready to ticket them for illegal parking.

In the next few seconds, Ross realized that this world, whatever else it might be, was most definitely designed for Commander Freff, not for Ross Allen. As Ross watched, the driver of the car pointed at them with the device he had removed from his belt. There was a hiss from the object and a sizzling sound next to Ross. He looked over just in time to see what was left of Joe Kujawa toppling off the bulldozer.

Ross wasn't consciously thinking of anything, even

31

survival, as he dived headfirst over the back of the seat and the fuel tank behind it. He landed with a thud on one side, the breath knocked half out of him. He glanced back at the bulldozer in time to see the top half of the exhaust pipe vanish to the accompaniment of another sizzling sound.

From somewhere Ross got the breath to scramble up. As long as he crouched slightly, the bulldozer blocked the other man and his weapon, unless the thing could blast through several tons of steel as easily as it had through Kujawa and the exhaust pipe. Keeping as low as he could, Ross sprinted back along the driveway and into the underbrush. When he was a few yards into the brush, he heard another spasm of crackling and sizzling, and a patch of foliage several yards behind him vanished.

Heedless of limbs and vines, Ross fought his way through the growth, tripping and falling every few yards, sometimes crawling, sometimes running. Twice more nearby bushes sizzled into nothingness as the fire from the alien weapon struck them. The noise he was making was obviously giving away his position, but if he tried to be quiet his pursuer could probably catch him in moments. He had to do something, fast, or join Kujawa as another victim. But what was there to do, besides run? Communicate? When someone shoots at you on sight, it makes meaningful communication somewhat difficult.

He wondered briefly about the old theory that any race advanced enough to have this kind of science would automatically have solved the problem of violence. It appeared to be disproved.

Another crackle, to his right and behind him, forced

him sprawling to his left. There had to be something he could do—there had to be!

Then he remembered the dynamite.

Suddenly, there was hope. But not too much. What could he do with dynamite? Throw it at his pursuer? To do that, he would have to be within easy range of that weapon, which could apparently vaporize both the dynamite and himself before either could be effective. Besides, a stick of dynamite flying through the air with a burning fuse is not only obvious but pretty easy to avoid. Commander Freff, of course, could cut the fuse and time it like a hand grenade, and do so while he was running, but Ross was realizing more and more every second that he wasn't Commander Freff. He wasn't even sure he could throw the stuff far enough to escape the blast himself, and fuse lengths were a total mystery. He'd used dynamite occasionally on construction jobs, but it didn't make a lot of difference if your fuse was a bit long, there. The rock wasn't going to run away from you, or shoot back.

Something crackled behind him again, a bit closer this time. A new surge of desperation shot through him. Whatever he was going to do, he'd better do it soon. His pursuer was a lousy marksman, but he couldn't keep missing forever.

A wall appeared through the undergrowth. Must be the building. Could he get back inside? Maybe if he could then so could his pursuer and he'd be in a real trap inside that vast open room. Stand just inside the door, maybe, and clobber his pursuer as he came through? Possibly, if nothing better occurred to him.

He skirted the ramp and peered down it. The wall at the bottom was solid, without a break. It must have closed automatically after the bulldozer. Running down the ramp might cause it to open again, but then again, it might not. He shivered at that thought and rushed on, noticing that the undergrowth thinned out near the building. As he dodged behind one of the larger trees, a limb crackled into nothingness where he had been a moment before.

With a burst of strength he hadn't thought he possessed, Ross added to his speed and raced around the corner of the building. *Now or never,* he thought, and stopped abruptly, just a few feet past the corner. Trying to remember how fast a fuse burned, he yanked one of the sticks of dynamite from his belt, and his pipe lighter from his pocket. Thank heavens, he thought, for old habits. If Sheryl had succeeded in her campaign to get him to stop smoking a year ago, he'd probably have quit carrying the lighter by now. Hastily he lit the fuse and watched it for a second. It wasn't burning very fast, and he could hear footsteps approaching the corner.

Quickly he moved the lighter to a point closer to the cap. Suddenly the fuse seemed to be burning with alarming speed; he dropped it and ran. The vegetation was still thin here, so he sprinted desperately to get out of sight before his pursuer rounded the corner, and to get behind a tree before the dynamite went off.

Abruptly, the footsteps and crackling of bushes which marked his pursuer's progress halted. The other man must have reached the clear area near the building, and was probably standing at the corner, taking careful aim at Ross's unprotected back, which tingled in anticipation. Ross dived sideways into the vegetation, rolling through the brush until he was sheltered behind the broad white trunk of one of the tropically-leaved trees. Then he pulled another stick of dynamite from his belt and tried to peer around the tree, back toward his pursuer. The first stick had missed; it hadn't exploded yet, and the pursuer must have either gone past it by now or stopped and pinched out the fuse. Maybe he could light a second stick, this one with only a fraction of inch of fuse, and heave it out of the thicket at the sound of pursuit. If he could just time it correctly. . . .

Behind him was only silence. Why wasn't the other man pounding down the path toward him? Why hadn't that dynamite gone off? His pursuer must have pinched out the fuse; maybe while he was doing that, he had lost sight of Ross?

Ross knew that logically, he should keep perfectly quiet. If his pursuer had lost track of him, the surest way to have the track picked up again was to move. But the suspense of waiting without knowing where the other man was or what he was doing was was too much to bear. Ross shifted slightly and craned his neck in an effort to find an opening he could see through. Cautiously, he moved away from the tree, listening and looking.

Finally, he found an opening in the brush and peered through. He blinked and shook his head in disbelief. The other man was standing a few feet from where the dynamite must be lying, paying it no attention at all. Instead, he was facing the wall of the building, staring at it.

Ross didn't understand what was going on, but he did realize that his opponent was so preoccupied with the building that he probably hadn't even seen the dynamite. Trying to be perfectly quiet, Ross started back toward the big tree. He had just reached it when the dynamite went off. The sound of the explosion was almost deafening, and Ross's ears rang ferociously. His lighter had been blown out. He pocketed it and stuffed the unused stick of dynamite back in his belt. His hands, he noticed, were shaking again.

What kind of man, he wondered, would stand and stare at a blank wall while ignoring a sputtering stick of dynamite in plain sight only a few feet away? Someone who had never seen a stick of dynamite before?

Or someone who had never seen a wall before?

Ross threaded his way back out of the bushes and walked slowly back along the wall. There was less left of his late pursuer than there had been of Kujawa. He must have been standing almost directly over the dynamite. Ross stared at the remains in a sort of horrified fascination, held in the same way as one's gaze is held by a photograph of the St. Valentine's Day Massacre, or of a battlefield.

He noted minor details. The clothing seemed to be a one-piece uniform. The belt held a pouch of moderate size, apparently empty. For holding the gun?

Being reminded of the gun enabled Ross to shake himself back to some sort of purpose. He could use that gun, if he could find it. A world where your first contact shot at you without even asking questions was a world where you weren't going to last long without a gun. It had been in the man's right hand, but the right hand was no longer attached to the body. Ross forced himself to look away from the form at his feet and search for missing parts. He was still shaking, though not as much. Killing someone wasn't nearly as impersonal an event as the depictions on the movie screen implied.

After a minute, he found the gun. It was in the edge of the brush, a few yards past where Ross had been hiding. It was still clutched in the severed hand. Slowly, trying not to look at what he was doing, Ross squatted down and pried the fingers loose. Strangely, there was no blood on the weapon.

With the gun in his hand, the muzzle carefully pointed away from himself, Ross hurried back along the building, looking down only enough to avoid the body. By the time he reached the ramp and the driveway, the shaking was almost gone, externally at least.

As he walked along the driveway toward the bulldozer, he held the gun up to inspect it. As far as he could tell, it was undamaged. There was a grip for the hand, a slightly raised ridge on the front of the grip that could be a recessed trigger, and a thick triangular barrel. Ross could find no method of reloading the weapon, or even a hole in the end of the barrel. The muzzle was somewhat discolored; that was all. The entire weapon was black, with the only marking being a football-shaped light yellow area on the bottom of the grip. That is, it was mostly light yellow. One end of the football, perhaps a tenth of the total area, was dark red. To his touch, the colored area was indistinguishable from the rest of the surface. An identification symbol? Or perhaps a charge indicator of some sort? He couldn't tell.

Taking the weapon in one hand, he tried sighting with it. There were no sights as such, but one could sight along the top of the triangular barrel. Perhaps, Ross thought, that explained why his pursuer had beeen so remarkably inaccurate. The grip was remarkably uncomfortable, and after a moment he saw why. It was neatly grooved to fit two more fingers than he happened to own. Fingers much more slender than his, as well. Strange; he distinctly recalled prying loose the normal number of fingers when he acquired the weapon.

Ross stopped and sighted as best he could toward one of the white trees several yards down the drive. He pulled lightly at what he assumed was the trigger, but nothing happened. He squeezed harder, and he wondered if possibly the yellow football shape might be a safety catch of some sort. He poked at it, with no result. Maybe the weapon had been damaged in the explosion after all. He shook it, tapped it on one side with his knuckles. Not having the slightest idea of how it worked was a distinct disadvantage in any attempt to repair a flaw. He sighted on the tree again, and again squeezed the trigger.

Nothing happened, and he increased the pressure, putting all the strength of his hand into the grip. The trigger slid back into the grip, and there was a faint hissing sound. The discolored area at the muzzle glowed, and a large circular section of the tree crackled and disappeared.

Ross quickly released the trigger, which immediately slid back into place. He looked at the yellow football on the grip, but there was no change as far as he could tell. He started to tuck the gun under his belt, but not only was the triangular barrel very uncomfortable but the trigger was pressing against the belt. Considering the force required to move the trigger it didn't seem too dangerous, but considering what the gun would do to him if it did happen to go off he decided to remove it. He wished briefly that he had taken the belt and pouch that went with the gun, but he could stick it in his pocket just as easily. Going back to get the pouch would just be an excuse to avoid returning to the bulldozer.

And to Joe Kujawa's body.

He put the gun in his pocket and walked toward the idling bulldozer.

He was finished in an hour. He had no digging tools and was a little afraid to try the gun out on the ground, but Kujawa's body was out of sight in the brush and covered with as many branches and rocks as he could locate. The bulldozer was backed down the ramp, out of sight of the road, and properly shut down, in case he should ever need it again. The last thing he had done was to open the bulldozer's tool box and take out the small briefcase he normally carried there. It had contained his empty lunch sack, a couple of paperbacks, and half of a manuscript, all of which had been dumped into the toolbox. Into the briefcase had gone the remaining sticks of dynamite and half a dozen small tools. Sight of the dynamite had threatened to bring back the shakes. He had been running through the jungle, falling down, banging into trees, and all the time carrying in his belt several sticks of dynamite with blasting caps and fuses attached. It was a wonder that he hadn't blown himself up in that first fall, or that Joe hadn't taken both of the other men with him when he toppled off the bulldozer.

With his chores accomplished, Ross took a last look around and walked down the driveway. Thoughts of Joe's family alternated with thoughts of his own future on this planet. Both seemed equally depressing.

The alien vehicle was still hovering over the road, hissing quietly. The section which had vanished to let the driver out had not reappeared. Ross approached it cautiously, wondering why there had been no more traffic on the road. Surely such a well-constructed road indicated a fair volume of traffic, but it wasn't visible. He peered inside the car, wondering if he should get in. A car seemed obviously a superior form of transportation, but could he operate it? Commander Freff would have had no trouble, but Commander Freff was beginning to seem irrelevant to Ross's problems.

The interior of the car was small, and Ross could see no controls of any kind. There was simply a pair of contour chairs, which didn't seem to be contoured for the human anatomy. After a long hesitation, Ross climbed in and slid into what he hoped was the driver's seat and began to search in earnest for anything that remotely resembled a control.

As he looked, the missing side of the car abruptly reappeared. Ross grabbed for it, trying to prevent it from closing, but he was too late. It had been too late, he suspected, the instant he had climbed inside. The door was closed before he had been able to react, but he continued the motion anyway. His hand didn't quite reach the door. Instead, it bounced off something invisible a fraction of an inch from the glass.

Suddenly, there was motion. Ross felt nothing, as though he was being insulated from the effects of acceleration, but his eyes reported that the car had spun around sharply and begun shooting rapidly back down the road. *Now,* Ross thought, in a somewhat grimmer mood, *we're really off to see the Wizard.*

CHAPTER 3

He was, Ross thought, being remarkably calm under the circumstances. In the last two hours, he had been snatched off Earth, seen his only link with Earth destroyed, seen his companion killed and in turn had killed the assassin, and was now helpless in an alien machine speeding toward an unknown and probably deadly destination. In fact, it probably wasn't calmness at all; he was simply numb.

Whatever it was, it allowed him to think. The logical thing to do was to try to find the controls of the machine he was in. In his initial search, he had touched only a few spots on the blank panel where the dashboard should have been; possibly he had activated something without meaning to. Now he began trying to relocate those spots to see if he could reverse whatever process he had started. He immediately realized that even if he could relocate them, it wouldn't do him any good. He couldn't touch the panel. His hand and probing finger was stopped short a fraction of an inch away, just as it had been stopped short of the door. It was like trying to force two magnets of the same polarity together.

He drew his hand back and jabbed forward sharply, one finger extended. The finger stopped just short of the panel, and for a moment he felt his entire hand and half of his arm gripped by an unseen force. He tried similar moves against the roof and both sides, and got similar results.

41

If he couldn't control it, maybe he could wreck it. He pulled the alien gun from his pocket and looked around, wondering where the car might have a vital spot. The way things had been going, he'd probably disable the gadget that opened the door, but he had to take the chance. The way the foliage was whipping past the windows, it wasn't going to take long for the car to reach its destination, no matter where that might be.

Before trying to shoot the controls, though, perhaps he should try the windows. That way, if the thing ever slowed down enough, he might have a chance of getting out. He pointed the weapon toward the far side of the car and, still with a certain difficulty, pulled the trigger.

At first he thought nothing had happened, but then he noticed that a series of charred spots was appearing in the wall of growth along the side of the road. He released the trigger, and the charred spots stopped appearing. He lowered the weapon toward an opaque part of the door and squeezed the trigger again. With the pistol pointed down, he couldn't see what was happening outside, but obviously nothing at all was happening to the door.

That seemed to be that. Clarke's third law—"Science, sufficiently advanced, is indistinguishable from magic,"—occurred to him. He had used the principle often enough in his fiction, but he had never expected to run into it in his own life.

The road abruptly entered a park-like area, minus the tin cans. The bushes and vines between the trees were replaced by a tall, coarse grass, and the trees, still with those odd white trunks, had much smaller leaves, hardly larger than those of an Earthly maple. The car stopped. There was little feeling of deceleration and no time spent on it; the vehicle simply shifted from top speed to zero. The door sections on both sides of the car vanished just as suddenly. Ross grabbed his briefcase from the outer seat and literally threw himself out of the car. Operating only on instinct, he ran frantically for the nearest trees, perhaps a hundred feet from the road. The heavy grass slowed him, dragged at his feet and legs, and his heart was thumping almost audibly by the time he reached the first tree. Without a thought, he ducked behind it and collapsed, his back against the trunk.

For a minute he sat there, breathing heavily, listening. The only sounds were the hissing of the car, a faint sighing of the breeze through the grass, and a few vaguely bird-like noises from the tree above him. He thought briefly of food, and wondered where his next meal was coming from. It had been only three or four hours since lunch, but he was definitely hungry and beginning to be desperately thirsty. And dirty. All the running and crawling he had done had taken its toll. His clothing was torn in a dozen places, and he felt at least two dozen bruises and scratches. His side was sore where he had landed in his dive off the bulldozer, and his left ankle felt as though it had been twisted.

He wondered briefly when all this had happened. He hadn't felt anything when it occurred. It was only now, while he could relax and take stock of himself, that it became evident. It was also now that he began to realize how incredibly lucky he had been so far. The assassin had shot Joe first, and then begun missing his target, and finally stood still long enough for Ross's dynamite to work. No other assassins had come along the road while Ross had been moving Kujawa's body and the bulldozer, and, amazingly, no one had been waiting here to zap him the moment he stepped out of the car. It was almost enough to convince him that someone really was up there looking after him the way he looked after Commander Freff.

"Make no sudden moves," a rich baritone voice said authoritatively from somewhere behind and to his left.

I might have known it wouldn't last, he thought. He considered trying to grab the alien gun in his pocket, but realized that pulling a gun when he couldn't even see his opponent would probably prove fatal. Besides, the owner of the voice hadn't shot at him yet, which was an improvement over his first encounter on this belligerent planet. He noticed the voice was speaking the same language as the one that had decorated the murals in the Gate building, and even had time to wonder how he knew that the written and spoken forms had the same source.

"Where is Raka?" the voice inquired.

"Who is Raka?" Ross asked, afraid that he already knew the answer.

Another voice broke in, a rasping, growling buzz that Ross understood with difficulty. "Presumably," it said, "this one did not know Raka well enough to exchange identification. We refer to the humanoid who originally possessed the vehicle in which you arrived—and the weapon in your pocket, which you have very wisely decided not to reach for."

Ross's hand twitched toward his pocket, but he restrained himself. He was silent for several seconds, but could think of no story that would hold together and do him any good. Before he could lie plausibly, he would have to know the ground rules, and he didn't even know what the game was. Might as well tell the truth and get it over with.

"He's dead," he said, tensing for whatever was to come.

The first voice cursed feelingly for a moment, then went on. "That fool was our only contact! I knew we shouldn't have let him go; he wasn't to be trusted." The voice continued with a string of sounds in neither the language of the Gates or English. From the tone, Ross judged they were more curses, and hoped they were directed against Raka and not himself.

"Where are you from?" the voice continued after a brief pause. "How long have you been here?"

"I'm from Earth," Ross said, and then realized that in this language, "Earth" translated to "Venntra" and referred to the dirt under his feet, the home planet. "From, uh, Sol Three," he corrected himself. "I've been here only a few . . . that is, a small part of this day." The units of time in his new language weren't related to the planet's revolution, and he found that he had no idea what length of time each word represented.

"He seems safe enough," the second voice rasped.

"All right," the first voice said. "You can get up."

Ross rose and looked around, hoping that the owner of the second voice didn't look as bad as he sounded.

He did. His posture was upright; he was bipedal and reptilian. The skin was an almost glistening greenish blue, and the head looked like that of a miniature— and not too miniature at that—tyrannosaur. Teeth, more nearly human than the rest of the features, were visible, and a bony crest ran from just above the eyes completely over the top of the head. The face was so totally alien that Ross could not read whatever expression it held. The only clothing was a wide belt with numerous pouches hanging from it. Ross wasn't even sure that the creature was male, though thinking of it as "he" somehow felt right. He was rather casually holding a twin to the gun that Ross still had in his pocket. The grip fit his slender, seven-fingered hand perfectly.

The owner of the other voice was something else again. She was very definitely mammalian and female, and stood perhaps an inch taller than Ross's own six feet. Her skin was nearly black, though there was a faint russet tone to it where the light struck it just right, and her hair, hacked off at about shoulder length, was a brilliant red. The features were closer to Nordic than any other type Ross could think of, though perhaps size and build had something to do with that judgment. She was dressed in something that resembled slacks and a sweater, but both were made of some greenish fur. She was in the act of lowering a bow and arrow which had been pointed at Ross. Across her shoulder was a quiver of arrows.

"We recognize the weapon in your pocket, of course," the reptile said. "But that other container there," he indicated the battered briefcase. "Does that contain weapons?"

"Just tools," Ross said firmly.

The alien cocked his head sideways and studied Ross for a moment. "I sense there is something else there that you do not wish us to know about," he said.

The woman grabbed for the briefcase, but the reptile waved her away. "It is all right," he said. "This one does not fully trust us yet." He replaced the gun in its pouch. "We, however, need have no misgivings about him."

The woman frowned in obvious disagreement, but said nothing.

Ross shrugged. What was this saurian, anyway, a

mind reader? "All right," he said. "It's not really a weapon, but I do have some explosives in there."

The saurian's head made a slight circular bobbing motion, and Ross wondered if it was the alien equivalent of a self-satisfied nod.

"My name is Orl," the alien said. "This is Kari," he added, indicating the woman. "And you?"

"Ross Allen," he said, resisting the impulse to try shaking hands.

The alien again made the circular bobbing motion. At the same time, the thin, almost nonexistent lips moved back farther, revealing more of the teeth. These were not as human-like as Ross had first thought. There were a lot more of them, for one thing, and they seemed to be pointed or serrated.

"Rossallen will be of help to us," Orl said to Kari. "Not in the same way as Raka, but I have the feeling that there is something about him we will find useful."

"If you say so," Kari muttered, obviously unconvinced, and swung to face Ross. For the moment she seemed more menacing than Orl. "Why did you kill Raka?" she demanded abruptly.

Ross swallowed and backed away a step. Yes, she definitely looked more dangerous than Orl. For one thing, she seemed perpetually angry, and for another, she kept fingering the huge bow she had slung over her shoulder, as though hoping for a chance to use it on someone.

Ross explained what had happened, dwelling particularly on the fact that Raka had shot first.

"I knew it," Kari said when he finished. "I should have gone with him. Raka was too superstitious to be trusted, and he had the attention span of a gnat!"

Orl made a terrifying sound, and Ross looked toward him with a start. Kari merely frowned.

"I don't see that it's at all funny," she said.

So that was alien laughter. Ross shivered slightly and wondered what a bellow of rage would sound like.

"You are correct, of course," Orl said, regaining his composure. He turned to Ross. "Before Raka attacked you, did you see a similar vehicle pass by?"

"I didn't see anything," Ross said, "because I couldn't see the road. I heard something that might have been one of your vehicles."

Kari's frown deepened. "We'd better get out of here, then," she said. "Since Raka let him get away, he'll be back soon with a whole squad of them."

Orl twitched slightly; possibly his equivalent of a shrug, Ross thought, or perhaps a shudder.

"Presumably correct," Orl said, and turned to Ross. "We had been seen by one who was not friendly. Raka pursued him, but allowed himself to become distracted by your arrival and allowed the dangerous individual to escape. We will therefore establish ourselves in a new location." He paused a moment. "You will, of course, be most welcome to accompany us."

Orl and Kari both started toward the road, where the car still waited. Ross followed. There was no other choice. They had not tried to kill him out of hand, Orl seemed relatively civilized despite his appearance, and they seemed to have at least some idea of what was going on, and maybe even some ideas on what to do about it.

As they drew near the car Orl gestured, somewhat like a reptilian Mandrake, and the door-sections, which had been solidly closed as they approached, vanished again. Ross started to protest that there wouldn't be enough room for all three of them, but before he said anything he glanced inside and saw that there was room. Instead of the cramped space in which he had ridden here, there was a roomy interior containing three seats.

As Ross settled himself, the door sections reappeared and the car rose about a foot farther off the ground and swung off the road. As it zigzagged to avoid trees, Ross couldn't be sure whether it was responding to Orl's hands hovering over the blank panel before him or whether it had some built-in avoidance system.

"As long as we stay clear of the roads," Orl explained, "we should have no trouble. From what I have seen, the local barbarians have not learned to operate the cars anywhere but on the road."

For a time, they drove in silence. Orl kept his eyes forward, while Kari kept peering out the back. Ross had a thousand questions, but he had the feeling that he shouldn't disturb Orl's driving concentration, since the trees were becoming thicker.

Eventually the trees began to thin out and they found themselves on the edge of grassy plain that seemed to stretch on forever. Some of the tension seemed to leave Orl, and he glanced at Ross.

"I assume you are confused, since you were brought here unexpectedly."

Ross nodded. "Totally ignorant would be a better description. For a start, could you tell me where we are?"

"With respect to your home world? No, there is no way to tell that."

Ross felt a sinking feeling. "But you seemed to know about the Gate. You weren't surprised when I told you how I got here."

"Of course not. That is how both Kari and I arrived here, too."

"You mean you're not natives?" The sinking feeling deepened. "But you can drive the cars; that gun fits your hand." A thought struck him. "Raka, then? Was he a native?"

"In a manner of speaking," Orl said. "Raka was born on this planet, which Kari and I were not. His ancestors, however, undoubtedly came through one of the Gates."

"Oh." Ross considered this for a moment. "Then where are the natives?"

"As far as Kari and I have been able to learn, there are none any more. With respect to your comment about the weapon fitting my hand, my ancestors originally did live on Venntra, and the natives, if there were any left, would look somewhat like myself."

"But if your ancestors. . . ." Ross shook his head. "Maybe I'd better stop asking questions and let you explain everything."

Orl's lips twitched in what Ross hoped was a smile. "Since I do not know everything, I find myself unable to explain it. However, my ancestors emigrated from this planet about two hundred of our generations ago. I am not sure whether this was the home world of our race or merely one of the major centers of our empire; the records are unclear. All travel between worlds was through what you call the Gates."

"The magic flat stones," Kari explained.

"Matter transmitters of some kind," Ross said, and Orl made another of the terrifying sounds that apparently were his laughter. Kari glared at Orl but said nothing. Ross, realizing what the saurian was laughing at, vowed to keep any future scientific rephrasing of Kari's comments to himself.

"From your viewpoint, magic is probably the more

accurate term," Orl said when he had subsided, and Kari shot a triumphant look at Ross.

"As I was saying," Orl continued, "all travel was by means of the Gates. One assumes that star ships must have been used at one time; it would seem necessary to reach a world through normal space in order to set up the Gates themselves. But we have no records of star ships.

"My world, Elsprag, was in the process of being colonized. Shortly after the first contingent of colonists came through, the Gate from Venntra was closed. A number of the colonists, it is reported, returned to discover what the problem was, but . . ."

"I thought you said the Gate was closed," Ross interrupted.

"The Gate from Venntra to Elsprag was closed. The Gate from Elsprag to Venntra remained open, and was used to send a few colonists through to discover the problem. When none of them returned to Elsprag, we closed that Gate as well, and it was only reopened when I was sent through it."

"Then each Gate only goes one way?" *No wonder,* Ross thought, *we couldn't find any controls to reverse it. There weren't any.*

"Of course," Orl said. "It takes two gates, one for each direction, to make a complete link."

Hope spurted through Ross like a shot of adrenalin. Two Gates! Then the gate from Venntra to Earth still existed!

"The second Gate, the one from Venntra to Earth—where is it?"

"It could be anywhere," Orl said. "The Gates have to be separated by a considerable distance."

"But don't you have any way of finding it?"

51

"Possibly. I have a somewhat incomplete map of Venntra as it existed two hundred generations ago, copied from our records. Gate locations are marked, but not identified as to where each Gate leads. There is a possible means of identifying the Gates that we may be able to find here on Venntra, but of course, considering the length of time involved, many Gates may have been destroyed. They may even have been destroyed deliberately; we do not know why or how they were closed."

"What about the other Gate to Elsprag? You didn't come here without knowing that you could return, did you?"

"But of course I did. I know the location of the Gate to Elsprag, and I have some knowledge of how to reopen it. But I will not reopen it until I have knowledge of what caused it to be closed in the first place. It must have been a tremendous threat to our civilization, and I must be sure that it no longer exists."

"A war . . ." Ross began.

"Unlikely," Orl stated. "There had been no wars on Venntran worlds for hundreds of generations."

"Such powerful magicians," Kari commented sagely, "would have no need to fight among themselves. Each could command whatever he wanted."

Orl laughed slightly. "That is quite true, in a manner of speaking."

Ross shook his head in frustration. To know that the Gate to Earth might still exist, and to be able to do nothing about the fact, except wait!

"Why did you wait so long to return?" he asked.

"When our first ventures failed, it was illogical to continue to waste manpower until Time was given a chance to operate. Our colony had little more than three hundred people when the Gate was closed. We needed all of them."

"But two hundred generations?"

"When the Gate closed, we were cut off from all supplies, information, and further colonists. Three hundred people is not a great number with which to rebuild a civilization. It required time."

"But you had advanced scientific knowledge," Ross protested.

"Scientific knowledge is of little value without the technology to make use of it." Orl gestured at the vehicle. "Of what use is it to have all the required knowledge to construct such a vehicle if one does not have mining machinery for obtaining metallic ores? We had the advantage of knowing precisely what needed to be accomplished, but it still required a great deal of time, even to build up the population sufficiently so that the work could be attempted."

Ross nodded reluctantly. Orl was right. No scientist, even if he had all the knowledge of Earth, could have built an integrated circuit or a vacuum tube in 1,000 B.C. Having the knowledge without the equipment must have been frustrating for those early Elsprag settlers. He thought of a question that had occurred to him before.

"Why did Venntra have a Gate leading to Earth, anyway? We weren't colonized. Our archaeologists would have found traces of it."

"As they found traces of the Gates?" Orl asked slyly. "However, you are correct. There were, according to one of our old books, many worlds devoted to tourism." The word Orl used did not translate strictly as "tourist", Ross realized. There was the implication of vacations and sightseeing, but also implications of scientific observation and serious study. "Some of the tourist worlds were eventually colonized," Orl continued, "but there were always more worlds than colonists."

Suddenly, Ross quit paying attention to Orl's explanations. There was someone watching him. He looked around sharply and saw nothing. Outside the car the grassy plain continued. In the distance he could see another stand of trees, and beyond that a range of mountains rose into the crystal clear sky. In all the area he could see, there was no sign of life.

The feeling persisted and grew stronger.

"Where are we going?" Ross asked, his voice sharper than he had intended. Kari looked at him curiously.

"To another Gate," Orl replied. "According to my map, there is a Gate not too far distant. If it is as well preserved as the one through which you came, we should be able to have all our immediate needs provided for."

Ross paid little attention to the explanation. The feeling of apprehension was growing within him. Something terrible was about to happen.

"Don't you feel anything?" he asked, his voice loud in the enclosed space.

"I sense nothing wrong, if that is your meaning," Orl said.

The frown on Kari's face deepened and she darted a look first toward Ross and then out the rear of the car.

"Stop the car!" Ross all but shouted.

"For what reason, Rossallen?" Orl's voice sounded more menacing than ever.

"I don't know! But you've got to stop!"

Orl was silent, turned partly in his seat to watch Ross and Kari. Kari sat silently, but her frown was deepening until it bordered on a ferocious scowl. Her eyes darted continuously from one window to another, and her fingers worked nervously at her longbow, wedged into the seat beside her.

Ross saw none of this. His only concern was the fear that was growing within him, the feeling that someone was watching him, was waiting for him somewhere out there. The watcher, whoever or whatever it was, sat waiting to pounce and destroy him, slowly, completely, and horribly.

He had to stop the car! He *had* to, before it was too late!

CHAPTER 4

The car was not going to stop, Ross realized, until he was dead. Or until *he* stopped it! The terror boiled up within him, and he lunged forward, grasping blindly at Orl. The saurian dodged, bringing one hand up to defend himself. Kari brought her left hand around sharply. The back of it struck Ross solidly across the jaw, knocking him backward into the seat.

He lay there for a moment, partially stunned but still feeling the terror that drove into him. She was in with them! Whatever lay ahead, waiting for him, she was a part of it! He struggled to shift his weight and reach the gun in his pocket.

"Rossallen!" Kari's deep voice filled the interior of the car, and her left hand grasped his wrist. Her fingers felt like steel, and despite his struggles he couldn't move his arm toward the pistol. His other arm was pinned between his body and the edge of the seat.

"Orl," she snapped, turning to the saurian. "Do as he says. Stop the car."

Orl hesitated a moment, then turned back to the control panel. His hands darted across it briefly, and the car stopped, settling a few inches downward.

Ross continued to struggle. Now that the car was stopped, whatever it was out there waiting for him had only to come and get him. Kari was in league with it; she'd see that it got into the car, and hold him captive until. . . .

Ross's mind veered away from that thought, afraid to even think about what would happen to him then.

Then, as he struggled to break free of her grip, the thought of Commander Freff emerged from somewhere and, unwelcome, forced its way into his mind. His own fear was terrible enough by itself; there was no need for his subconscious to dredge up the Commander and compare Freff's heroic fictional reactions with Ross's real one! But his subconscious insisted on doing it. Freff would never let himself get into an idiotic situation like this, literally shaking in his boots from some overwhelming but indefinable fear, and held helpless by a single woman. Not Commander Freff. Freff would be in command in all situations; at the very least, he would be in command of himself.

The image of the noble Commander, clear-eyed and firm-jawed, swam before Ross's eyes. In the Commander's face Ross could see mirrored the terror in his own mind, but in Freff it was somehow contained. The Commander did not dissolve into a screaming, struggling child; he was above such vulgar displays.

Slowly, without fully realizing how he did it, Ross regained control of himself. The feeling of terror did not abate; he still knew that something lay waiting for him beyond the protective shell of the car. His entire body tingled, and he was sure that every muscle was trembling. But, gradually, despite its continued intensity, the terror lost its hold on him. Despite the fear that screamed all around him, he was able to think rationally and force himself to act. First, he had to stop struggling, before Kari was forced to break his arm. He gritted his teeth and willed his muscles to relax. He wasn't entirely sure how this worked, but the muscles gradually seemed to be getting the message, and his arm stopped trying to tear itself from Kari's grip.

"You—can—let—me—go—now." His voice, through clenched teeth, was barely intelligible. Willing his jaws to relax as well, he repeated the message.

Kari, he noticed, was showing signs of agitation herself. Her face was tense and, now that his wrist lay unmoving in her grip, he could tell that she, too, was trembling. Hesitantly, she removed her grip and concentrated on fighting her own inner battle.

"Turn around," Ross said to Orl, forcing his voice to be relatively steady. "Get us out of here."

"I do not understand what . . ." Orl began, but Ross cut him off.

"I don't, either! Just move this contraption, back the way we came! Fast."

In a seemingly slower, more deliberate manner than before, Orl's hands moved over the panel. The car lifted, spun about, and with what seemed like agonizing slowness, began to move back the way they had come, gradually picking up speed. Ross knew that it was all accomplished in a second or less, but it seemed like minutes.

Then, as if a giant hand had snatched a huge weight from his shoulders, the fear was gone. There was no gradual departure. One instant Ross was grimly willing himself to relax and not scream out the terror that was in him; the next instant he was actually relaxing and feeling as safe and secure as he had ever felt since he arrived on Venntra. He was, in fact, as limp as a dishrag. Kari, too, slumped noticeably and gave a sharp sigh. Only Orl seemed unaffected as he continued to control the vehicle with deliberate motions.

"What was that?" Ross asked. "What happened to us?"

Orl glanced at him. "I had hoped," he said, "that you could tell me. I could sense a great agitation in you, and a lesser one in Kari, but I felt none myself and could see no reason for yours."

"Neither could I, for that matter," Ross grinned weakly and turned to Kari. "You got a dose of it, too, didn't you?"

Kari nodded. "There was something out there, waiting to get us," she said.

"Did you get any clue as to what it was?" Ross asked.

She shook her head. "I don't know. But it was there."

"It was there," Ross agreed. "But as for what it was, or how I knew of it. . . ." his voice trailed off.

"A mental force of some kind, then," Orl said. "Interesting. Perhaps attuned to the human metabolism, since I felt nothing. This is something that our records never hinted at. I wonder. . . ." his voice also trailed off into thought.

The sun, Ross noticed as he lay back and looked out the car window, was no longer directly overhead, though it didn't seem to have moved very far down in the sky. He looked at his watch and saw that it was almost six o'clock, back on Earth.

Back on Earth. He repeated the phrase to himself, as if he was trying it out to see how it sounded. Strangely, it no longer overwhelmed him with longing. He was beginning to adjust to the fact that he was on Venntra for a long time; maybe for good, which he recognized was a good rational approach.

Before he could apply a great deal of good rational thought to all the implications of his situation, they crossed another Venntran road which ran at right angles to their path. Ross was observing it with interest when another vehicle came out of a dip several hundred yards to their left. As far as Ross could tell, it was identical to the one he was riding in.

Orl apparently noticed it, too, for his hands suddenly made a number of rapid moves over the blank panel in front of him, and the grass suddenly seemed to be moving past them much faster than before.

Looking out the back, Ross saw the other vehicle stop at about the point they had crossed the road. It hovered there for several seconds, receding in the distance as he watched. Abruptly, it left the road and rapidly accelerated along the path of their own car.

Strangely, now that there was something tangible for him to be afraid of, Ross felt quite calm. Perhaps, he thought, his fear circuits had been overloaded by his previous terror and hadn't fully recovered. After the incredible heights of terror that he had experienced only a few minutes before, the prospect of being pursued by a car full of killers gave rise to nothing more than a slight nervousness.

"I thought you said they couldn't drive those things off the road," he commented.

"The ones that chased us the other day couldn't—or didn't," Orl said. "This driver appears more capable, but our chances of escape are excellent once we reach that forested area ahead."

"It would be easier to stand and fight," Kari muttered.

"Perhaps so," Orl said, "but it is not practical. They are at least as highly skilled with their weapons as we with ours, and we have no idea how many may be in that vehicle. Don't forget, this race tends to run in packs."

Kari muttered rebelliously, but she subsided. Ross wondered if she was simply anxious for a fight to relieve the monotony of the ride, or if she perhaps felt impelled to prove to herself that the fear she had felt was a thing of the past and that she was as brave as she had ever been. Ross had never considered himself especially brave, so he felt no particular need to redeem himself now. Kari, though, was apparently a warrior, and that kind of paralyzing fear would perhaps have a humiliating effect that she needed to wipe out in her own mind.

"What's the range of these pistols?" Ross asked, fumbling in his pocket for his.

"Perhaps a hundred yards," Orl said. "They are still well out of range."

Ross looked back at their pursuers again. "I think they're gaining," he said.

"He's right," Kari agreed. "I told you we'd be better off to fight."

Orl adjusted a reflecting surface that evidently acted as a rear view mirror. "I see. Perhaps you were correct. We may be forced to fight, whether we want to or not.

Ross estimated the distance between the vehicles at about two hundred yards, and wished for a moment that he had a good rifle available. He'd killed deer at longer ranges than that. Although, once he thought about it, he realized there was no guarantee that a rifle bullet would do any damage to the pursuing car or its occupants.

What about dynamite, though? There was nothing to lose by trying, and even if the explosion failed to damage their pursuers there was a good chance that it would throw their vehicle out of control. A feeling of elation rose in him as he groped on the floor for his briefcase. Finally locating it, he fished out a dynamite stick. Still capped, he noted, and felt a small twinge in his stomach. He should have taken more care when he packed it; he must have been more excited than he remembered. Dynamite caps were nothing to get careless with, and they definitely weren't supposed to be in contact with the dynamite until just before an intended explosion.

Kari watched him with interest as he got out the lighter and eyed the fuse for several seconds. The last one had taken far too long to go off. He had decided on what he hoped was a suitable length and was about to light it when it occurred to him that he didn't know how to get the thing out of the car.

"Can you roll down a back window?" he asked Orl.

Orl glanced at him. "To what purpose?"

"So I can throw out something that may discourage them a little."

Orl eyed the explosive. "This is what killed Raka?"

"It is."

"Very well," Orl said, turning back to the control panel. "Tell me when you are prepared."

"Be sure and get the window open fast," Ross said. "Once I get this thing lit, I don't think I can stop it."

Ross noticed that Kari was fingering her bow again, as if she would like to get in a shot at the same time Ross threw out the dynamite. Could she fire an arrow that far? he wondered.

Ross lit the fuse, which started to burn with alarming speed.

"Now!" he shouted.

Orl's hands moved over the controls, but nothing happened.

"Now, I said!" Ross repeated.

"It is open, Rossallen," the saurian rasped. "Why are you waiting?"

"But . . ." For an instant, Ross stared at the back window, which still looked as solid as before. Then, with the fuse sputtering down to almost nothing, he threw the dynamite as hard as he could. It passed through the back window without a flicker.

Orls hands moved again, and a moment later an explosion jolted their vehicle savagely. For a moment, it tilted forward and seemed as if he was going to nose into the ground, but Orl played his hands frantically across the dash and the car righted itself and continued on its way.

Behind them, well in front of the pursuing vehicle, a huge geyser of smoke and dirt had erupted. The other car could be seen dimly behind the now-settling cloud. It seemed undamaged, but it had halted. The driver had evidently lost any ambition to pursue beings who could cause that sort of eruption.

As Ross turned back to the others, he noticed that Kari's eyes were wider than usual, and her mouth not as tightly shut as it normally was.

"Is that a common weapon on your world?" she asked, a slight touch of awe in her voice.

"More or less," Ross said. "It isn't actually a weapon, which is one reason it went off too close to the car. I'm not used to doing that sort of thing with it. Normally we use it for, uh . . ." Ross paused as he tried to find something in the language that would fit the idea. "To, uh, to dig holes with," he said finally.

Kari's eyes widened even more. He couldn't tell if she was being awestruck or simply didn't believe a word he said.

"It is very impressive to the primitive mind," Orl

said, "and therefore perhaps more useful to us than conventional weapons, which they have become familiar with during their residence here."

He spoke, Ross thought, like a landlord discussing the bad habits of a tenant who would be evicted in due time.

"Would it be possible, however," Orl continued, "for you to throw it a little farther if it becomes necessary to use it again?"

"I'll try," Ross said. "Actually it isn't a matter of how far I throw it; it's the length of the fuse that gives me trouble. I'll try to improve, though I hope there won't be a next time because I don't have a lot of the stuff left."

"You cannot make more?" Orl asked.

"Hardly. Our technology may not be as sophisticated as your Gates, but it still requires special equipment." As he spoke, Ross remembered stories in which characters had managed to make explosives by finding and mixing ingredients in a primitive world. Unfortunately, while he knew that the usual explosive made was black powder, he had no idea of what raw materials were required for it, much less how to find them. He ought to look that up when he got back to Earth; except when he got back, he wouldn't need to know.

Ross looked out the back of the car again. The cloud of dust was now well behind them and mostly dissipated, while their former pursuers were still sitting where they had stopped. He settled back, beginning to feel relaxed, at least in comparison to his feelings over the last few hours. Venntra was certainly no planet for anyone with a nervous disposition; Earth's so-called "rat race" of jobs and status was a pleasure jaunt compared to Venntra.

"I think I asked this before," he said, "but where are we going?"

"You did," Orl said without looking back. "You did not, however, seem to pay a great deal of attention to my answer. I am still attempting to reach a nearby Gate, probably much like the one from your Earth. Despite our temporary detour, we should be nearly there. Once we have reached it, if it is still in operating condition, our immediate needs will be provided for."

"There's more to it than just a Gate, then? Kujawa and I couldn't find anything at all."

"There is a great deal more," Orl replied, "if it is still operating."

"And you know how to make use of it?"

"Naturally," Orl replied. "It was designed by my race, after all."

"You don't think that perhaps two hundred generations on a colony planet might have changed your ideas of design a bit?"

"Of course not," Orl said, surprised. "Why should it?"

Ross noticed that his mouth was open, and closed it. Orl's race were evidently not greatly addicted to experiments, then. They'd probably get along fine with some of the instructors Ross had met in college.

"Once we're there, what then?" he inquired.

"Then," Kari announced, "we lay plans to recover Orl's magical equipment."

Orl rotated his head in the pattern that Ross was now equating with a nod. "That must still be one of our prime objectives."

"Magical equipment?" Ross inquired somewhat incredulously.

"Equipment for making magic," Kari explained.

"That's a big help," Ross told her, and she glowered at him.

"The scientific gear I brought through the Gate with me," Orl explained. "It was taken from me when I was captured."

"They actually capture people? I thought from Raka's reaction that they automatically shot newcomers on sight."

A ripple of motion moved across Orl's back. Another type of shrug? "Essentially, that seems to be correct. Apparently they do not want to share this world with anyone. I gather from Kari that this possessiveness is a common trait among humanoids, but I admit that I do not fully understand it. They do not kill newcomers from their own home world, but otherwise the only exceptions from the rule of instant death are creatures of my race. Raka said they are under orders from their leaders to bring anyone of my species back to their Temple. It seems unusual. No one from Elsprag has entered Venntra since long before the memories of any-one living here now, I suppose it is possible that my people from other cut-off colonies have occasionally ventured through a Gate, as I did, but Raka could re-member nothing of anyone ever seeing a creature like myself until I arrived. Yet the orders are apparently quite specific."

"But why?"

"I have no idea. Neither did Raka or any of his associates. They only knew their orders. The race is not overly individualistic. They did not even know the penalty for disobeying their orders, although it was rumored to be severe. Of course, since no one of my race seems to have appeared here for generations, there would have been no chance for disobedience, and the exact penalty might well have been forgotten. But it would seem logical that in that event, the orders would have been forgotten as well."

"It's certainly odd," Ross said. "Maybe you should have stayed with them and found out the answers."

"No," Orl said. "I suspect that I would not have lived long enough to learn. They were beginning to argue over whether or not the orders required that I be presented to their Temple alive, and the majority seemed to feel that it was unnecessary. Raka was one of the few who insisted on interpreting the orders literally."

"A strict constructionist," Ross murmured. "They do have their uses."

"I believe," Orl said, "that it was only the fear of being penalized if the others killed me that led Raka to aid in my escape."

"How did you manage to get away, now that you mention it? They don't seem the type to let prisoners go."

"Fortunately, Kari was nearby."

Ross looked skeptically at Kari. He had trouble imagining her taking Orl's side against humanoids; primitives were not notably tolerant of other forms of life.

"I'd run into Raka's people before," Kari offered, noticing the look. "I thought Orl was a demon of some kind—I'm still not sure he isn't—but by that time I was ready to help anything they were against." She shook her hair in what struck Ross as a totally out of place feminine gesture. "Besides, my clan totem on Leean looked something like Orl, so even if he was a demon he might be friendly to anyone from my clan. So I helped him. Even demons return favors sometimes," she finished.

"And you talked Raka into helping you?" Ross asked Orl.

"Not exactly. He was my personal guard, and he didn't try to kill me as soon as Kari attacked, which any of the others would have done automatically. A terribly violent people. Then Kari took him with us when we escaped, and he helped us after that. Or said he was helping us."

"He was the puniest of the lot and easiest to handle," Kari added, and looked condescendingly at Orl. "Orl did not even think of taking a prisoner."

"I am not accustomed to this sort of activity, I fear," the saurian admitted.

Kari laughed. "That's obvious. You always take a prisoner if you can, in strange country, so you can force him to give you information."

Ross winced at the casual reference to torture. "And Raka provided the information until I killed him, then."

"He provided information," Orl said. "I was never certain of how much of the information was truthful, however. I believe that he never quite gave up the idea of delivering me, alive, to his Temple. So when the humanoids in the other car spotted us and Raka insisted on following them to eliminate them as witnesses, I set the controls so that I could always recall the car no matter where he took it. While I am not accustomed to such casual treachery as you humanoids practice, I was provided with information on how to guard against it before I was sent here. Our records," he finished with quiet pride, "appear to be quite accurate concerning alien behaviour."

"Oh." Ross blinked. This seemed to be getting involved, and he rather suspected that he should be feeling insulted over that last comment. Besides, it didn't seem to have anything to do with Orl's equipment.

"Where are they keeping your magical equipment?" he asked. "Or do you know?"

"Raka said it would have been taken to the temple," Orl said. "I believe this was one of his truthful statements. It would seem logical that my captors, having lost their captive, should bring what they had left to the Temple. They might have thrown it away as useless, but Kari and I came back after they had left, and the instruments were not in the area. Thus the equipment was taken somewhere, and the Temple seems an obvious choice."

"Next question seems to be, what and where is this Temple?"

"The location is not too far from here. It is the headquarters of the barbarians who occupy Venntra. They seem to have a form of society in which the priests are also the rulers, and the Temple is the place where they receive instructions from their god. From Raka's description, I suspect that this god is in reality. . . ."

"A computer!" Ross interrupted, recalling dozens of stories in which computers ruled over the primitive descendants of its builders.

Orl produced his horrifying chuckle. "If it suits you to identify it as such, there is no harm in it. Kari would call it great magic, which is perhaps more accurate. At one time it controlled production and distribution of all material on Venntra, and operated power stations, Gates, and all forms of energy devices, as well as being a library, communication device, traffic controller, and some duties which seem to have no parallel on humanoid worlds."

Ross wondered what those might be, but Orl didn't

explain, and an earlier phrase had caught his attention.

"It operated the Gates?" he asked.

"It controlled the physical operation, and maintenance. Decision-making, of course, was in the hands of living members of my race."

"Then to open a Gate . . ."

"One orders the computer, as you call it, to make the proper adjustments. If it is still functional—which seems likely, in view of the continued operation of vehicles and incoming Gates—and if it recognizes the individual giving the order as one authorized to do so, then it will adjust the specified Gate to active status."

"Then the computer is really in control of this world, not Rakas people. And obviously, the reason these barbarians have orders to bring anyone of your species in alive is that the computer is looking for its masters!"

"The thought has occurred to me, Orl admitted. "However, it presumes that this computer has volition and purpose; that it, in short, thinks and plans much as we do. Our records do not show this to be the case. There are other possibilities. Perhaps the priests realize that the computer is a tool built by my species, and wish to learn more about how to use it. Kari assures me that if they desire knowledge from me, they have ways of insuring that I provide it. I do not propose to make any assumptions about the computer; I desire to obtain the facts before proceeding."

Ross nodded reluctantly. "I suppose you're right. But getting captured seems like such an easy way to get to the answers. How do we go about recovering your stuff without being captured?"

"Until Raka's unscheduled departure, we had hoped he would remain loyal to us—or to the power and riches we promised him—long enough to obtain the equipment for us."

Kari snorted. "You thought that. I thought he would keep it for himself, if he got it at all. Magical equipment is valuable."

"I do not think so,' Orl said. "He could neither have understood it nor used it. But that is of little consequence. It seems unlikely that we can trust any of the barbarians now. One of us must locate the equipment and return with it."

Ross frowned. "Wouldn't we be somewhat conspicuous?"

"I would certainly be unable to enter the Temple unnoticed," Orl said. "Kari might be able to disguise herself with material we can obtain at the Gate, though again it would be difficult, and women are not allowed a large role in the barbarian society, so she would find it hard to enter the Temple unobtrusively."

Kari shrugged. "I could kill the guards and the priests on duty. But doing it might attract attention."

Orl continued. "You, however, Rossallen, are not unlike Raka's people in general physical makeup."

"What? Wait a minute; I don't think I look all that much like them. And what about clothing? If they all wear those black uniforms. . . ."

"I believe we can provide you with one. I suspect they are used because they were a standard garment for humanoid visitors to Venntra, and that any Gates still in operation will provide them. The barbarians have no clothing factories; they must obtain the garments somewhere."

Ross gave up. If he was ever going to get off this crazy world, it seemed pretty obvious that Orl was going to have to help him. If he had to make like Commander

Freff, disguise himself as a member of an alien race and sneak into their temple to steal back another alien's magical equipment, so be it. After what had happened to him so far, it didn't even seem that terrifying.

He settled back and waited, watching more forest flow by on either side. Forest seemed to make up most of Venntra; the few cleared areas he had seen were relatively small. He glanced at his watch; nearly 6:30. He wondered how long the Venntran day was; it looked to be longer than Earth's, considering the distance the sun had moved in the time he'd been on the planet. Mostly, however, he wondered if the needs the Gate building supplied included a drink of anything and some food.

He must have dozed off, for the next thing he knew, the car was at a standstill at the bottom of a ramp that seemed identical to the one he had driven the bulldozer over just hours before. As he watched, Orl's hands played on the control panel of the car, and the wall before them vanished, revealing a room which at first glance was identical to the one at the Earth Gate.

But it was not the same. The room was lighted—had Orl done that when he opened the door?—and in the light he could see a half-dozen skeletons lying on the floor. They didn't appear to be human; they were too large, and didn't appear quite the correct shape, though that part was hard to tell.

The car moved through the opening and settled down near one wall. The doorway through which they had passed abruptly became a solid wall again. The side panels of the car disappeared, and Orl and Kari stepped out. Neither of them paid much attention to the skeletons, though Kari was alertly observant of the room in general. Orl tramped purposefully toward one wall, ignoring everything else.

72

After a brief hesitation, Ross followed his companions out of the car. Cautiously, he approached the center of the room, where three of the skeletons lay. As he approached, there were sounds, seeming to come from a great distance. He stopped and listened, but they appeared to be animal sounds, rather than anything produced by a civilization. They were coming from the air in the center of the room. Another Gate was still operating, after how many thousands of years? Another incoming Gate, from the evidence of the skeletons. Ross wondered if they had never found their way out of the Gate building, or if something else had killed them.

Lying next to one of the skeletons was a knife. It was crude, and the tip was broken, but it was made of metal. He looked more closely at the skeletons. The skulls were slightly less than human size, despite the greater size of the rest of the bones. Nearly seven feet tall, he thought, even though the legs seemed bowed slightly and the spine was curved. An intelligent ape? An Abominable Snowman from another world? He wondered if any more had entered Venntra. And why had no animals come through? He could hear scuffling sounds and grunting drifting through the Gate.

"Rossallen!"

It was Kari's baritone. Ross turned toward her and saw that she was standing in a small doorway in one side of the room. It hadn't been there when Ross got out of the car, but Orl had probably waved an arm and intoned the Elspragan equivalent of "Open, Sesame!" and there it was. As he walked to it, Ross looked idly at the murals that lined the walls of the building as they had the one from Earth. Most were the same, except that the one with the needle-like spire was missing, and one forest-mountain-and-lake scene that could have graced any Earth advertising for vacation spots had taken its place.

Inside the smaller room on the other side of the door, a bench made of the same greyish material as the walls ran along two of the walls. In front of the third wall was a higher ledge that must function as a table. A three-inch square of something, also grey, lay on the surface. As Ross entered, Orl picked up the square and bit off a chunk. Kari was standing next to the table, one hand pressed against a slightly darker triangle of material in the wall. When Ross looked back to the table, a second square of material lay there. This one was slightly yellowish in color, like a cake of compressed sawdust.

"Place your hand where Kari had hers," Orl instructed. "Your metabolism will be analyzed and sustenance provided."

Ross hoped that his square would look a bit more appetizing than the previous ones, but it didn't. The faint olive drab tint made it even less appealing, if possible. He decided that he was in no position to be picky; without Orl he might be outside, trying to trap animals or eating the alien equivalent of poison ivy. He picked the square up gingerly, finding it the approximate consistancy of styrofoam, hesitated a long moment, and took a bite. The taste was nonexistent, but somehow the dry, dessicated substance in his hand turned into a moist food with the consistency of thin cereal in his mouth, and the moisture felt wonderful in his throat. By the time he had finished the piece, he was no longer hungry or thirsty.

He was, however, terribly sleepy. Natural metabolism taking over, he supposed; he'd had a long, wearing day, and now he was fed, comfortable, and safe, and it was time to relax. He sat down on the bench and found that it was not the same marble-like substance which made up the floors and walls, but relatively soft and capable of shaping itself to his body. He was asleep in seconds.

When he was awakened by Kari's jabbing at his shoulder, it took him some time to recall where he was and how he had arrived. Mornings had never been a good time of the day for him, and this was no exception. But Kari was in no mood to pamper him.

"Orl worked some of his magic," she announced, holding out to him one of the black coveralls. When he made no move to take it, she grabbed one of his arms and hauled him upright. "Put it on," she demanded. "It will be dawn soon, and we want to observe the city today. When light comes, it will be too late to get close."

Ross took the coverall, which was as far as he could tell identical to the one Raka had been wearing. He wondered if it was his size, and looked around for some place where he could get dressed. There didn't appear to be one. Orl was not present, but the door was closed, and the room was barren of screens or any consideration for modesty. He thought of asking Kari to turn her back, thought what her probable answer would be, and decided that if she wanted to watch him dress, she could. She did, with a complete lack of interest that left him with a mixture of gratitude and chagrin.

The uniform fit perfectly. The material appeared similar to nylon or one of the other synthetics; Ross had never paid a lot of attention to clothing. Gradually his spirits lifted as Orl returned and they each pressed their hands against the mark in the wall. This time, instead of a single square, a kit containing several appeared. Each ate one, and carried the rest to the car, where Ross and Kari relaxed again while Orl maneuvered the vehicle out of the building and into the forest. Ross began to feel that the insanity they were setting out on had at least a chance of working. He didn't look all that much different from Raka, and Kari and Orl didn't seem to think the barbarians here were all that intelligent. He wouldn't have to be a perfect duplicate to fool them.

The sky, as perfectly clear as it had been the day before, was beginning to show signs of light when Orl brought the car to a stop in what appeared to be a dry creek bed. A hill, covered with the same white-trunked, large-leaved trees that had been around the Earth Gate, was on their right, away from the rising sun.

"The Temple city is over that hill," Orl said, pointing. The side panels of their car vanished and they climbed out.

"Kari and I have scouted this place before," Orl explained. "I can point out to you the building I believe to be the Temple. Kari and I will remain here until you return."

"And if I don't return?" Ross inquired.

"Then Kari and I will decide what to do next."

It wasn't, Ross thought, all that comforting a reply. Kari, who had started to lead the way up the hill, turned and grinned at him, and Ross rather surprisingly found himself reassured. Warrior societies, he recalled, generally placed great emphasis on aiding one's comrades. He tramped up the hill after her, with Orl in the rear, making more noise than both the humans combined. Kari was as silent as a ghost, and Ross had been on enough hunting trips to be a moderately good woodsman, but Orl was definitely a city type. When they were within a few yards of the top, Kari motioned Ross and

Orl to stop while she crouched down and eased herself slowly to the crest. A moment later, Ross heard her sharp intake of breath, and he tensed, half expecting a dozen black-clad barbarians to come pouring over the hill after them.

Nobody appeared, and Kari motioned them forward to join her. Ross copied Kari's motions and moved cautiously upward, stretching out beside her as he reached the top. Behind them, Orl lumbered up, keeping as low as he could. In front of them stretched a plain, dotted here and there with an occasional building, and apparently about a mile across from the hill they were on to a row of wooded hills on the far side. All the buildings were square and blocky and gray, though they varied considerably in size, one of them being considerably larger than any of the others. Milling around the buildings were hordes of black uniforms. Even at this distance their motions seemed aimless, like insects when a nest is disturbed. A number of the Venntran cars hovered quietly, and several of the barbarians were riding creatures which looked like a six-year-old's attempt at sculpting a horse.

"It's gone!" Kari announced in a loud whisper, staring at the plain.

"What's gone?" Ross inquired. There didn't seem to be anything out there that could have put that expression of amazement and fright on her face. Lots of the black uniforms, of course, but Orl had said this was a sort of government center, so that was to be expected.

"The city!" Kari said. "There were hundreds of buildings like those. It covered half the plain, all the way to those hills there." She turned to Orl. "What magic is this? How can even a powerful magician like you make an entire city vanish overnight?"

CHAPTER 5

"I couldn't," Orl said, and Ross wished he could fathom the expression on the saurian face.

"Are you sure this is the right place?" Ross asked.

"Of course," Kari responded. "It was not far from here where I rescued Orl."

"But on a strange world . . ." Ross began.

Kari's face turned into a mask of anger. "I may not know as much magic as you do, but I can still notice landmarks!"

Startled by the reaction, Ross stammered an apology, which was ignored.

"Fascinating!" It was Orl's rasping voice, only inches from Ross's ear, and for just a moment the tone sounded so familiar that Ross wondered how the saurian would go over on TV back on Earth.

"It would seem," Orl went on after a moment, "that the Temple remains intact. It is probably that large, square structure, the one fairly well out in the middle of the group."

"Any idea what happened?" Ross asked. "Could the barbarians have done it?"

Orl's head bobbed in a circular motion again, and Ross thought at first he was nodding. "It seems unlikely that they would have the power to do it intentionally, aside from the fact that they seem to be disturbed by it. No, this would seem more probably a clue to the force that originally closed the Gates—if I can interpret it."

Connecting the words with the head motion, Ross

realized that the latter had been in the opposite direction from the previous bobs; counterclockwise instead of clockwise. Given enough time, Orl might become as familiar to him as a human neighbor on Earth.

"Do you know what the other buildings are, or why they should be left after the city vanished?"

Orl circled his head negatively again. "Other than the Temple, I have no idea. Raka described the Temple, but none of the others. Since we do not know why most of the buildings vanished, we cannot understand why these did not, but it is of little importance. Our present expedition concerns only the Temple."

"Which is going to be even harder for me to reach," Ross commented, "with the barbarians swarming like ants down there. Is there any chance I could learn to operate that car? Walking in and out of that mess doesn't appeal to me."

Orl surveyed the vehicle thoughtfully, as it hovered above the creek bed a hundred feet below them. "It seems possible that you could learn to operate some of its simpler functions," he said. "Some of the barbarians have done so."

"Thanks for your confidence," Ross said acidly, but Orl merely looked puzzled and Ross had the distinct feeling that his sarcasm had been wasted. "That might be our best bet, then," he continued. "Get away somewhere to a place where I can practice driving. I don't suppose the world will end if we wait an extra day or two before getting your stuff."

"Any additional time spent here increases our danger," Orl said. "But I confess I have little hope of your being able to sneak into what remains of the city on foot. Therefore. . . ."

Orl was interrupted by Kari's yell. Ross saw her

fitting an arrow to her bow and then looked beyond her to see four black uniformed shapes coming at them through the trees to their left. Ross's first thought was to make a run for the car, but Kari was standing her ground. She was standing with feet solidly braced, bow drawn back, waiting for her best target. One of the approaching figures was reaching into a pouch, and Ross had the feeling that he knew what was going to be brought out of it.

"The one on the left!" he yelled at Kari, and then remembered he had a pistol of his own and grabbed it. Kari's arrow struck the barbarian on the left in the side, spinning him around and knocking him to the ground. One of the others dropped the spear he was carrying and dived for the fallen one's gun.

Ross fired, too quickly. The trunk of a tree to the left of the crouching barbarian sizzled and a large chunk disappeared from it. Almost simultaneously, several branches over Ross's head vanished as his opponent also fired too hastily. An arrow whispered past the barbarian's head close enough to make him duck and give Ross another chance. He must have just grazed his opponent; Ross could see no visible damage, but the man dropped the pistol, yelped in anguish, started to pick up the weapon and then changed his mind and took to his heels.

This seemed an eminently sensible idea to Ross. He glanced back toward the creek bed, wishing there was more cover between the car and their present location.

The car was gone.

Ross looked around frantically before he spotted it, only yards away, moving up the hill toward them.

"I shall maneuver the vehicle close to us,' Orl said. "Be prepared to get in when I open the doors."

Ross nodded and returned his attention to their attackers. The third was also down, with one of Kari's arrows protruding from his shoulder. Two more, both armed with spears, had appeared behind the original group and were moving up cautiously.

"We have no need to run from such as these," Kari said as she took aim with another arrow. She seemed to be enjoying herself.

"Perhaps not," Orl said, "but more are coming, and your missile supply is limited. Another car is approaching from the city."

The last of their original attackers hurled his spear at Kari, who dodged, and lunged for the fallen pistol. Kari loosed an arrow which grazed his arm and sent the gun spinning from his hand. As he turned to look for the weapon, Kari glanced at the approaching vehicle, which had now been joined by two more.

She shrugged. "Very well. I haven't enough arrows for all of them."

The car came to rest between them and the barbarians, and Orl clambered inside, with Ross at his heels. Kari lingered to shout a taunt at their attackers, and then reluctantly climbed into the car.

Orl didn't wait for them to get settled, but spun the car around and shot back down the creek bed the way they had come. The other vehicles separated, with the one in the lead descending into the creek bed after them and the others turning to follow along the hill. Watching them, Ross saw a half dozen of the barbarians on animalback, riding the same not-quite-horses he had seen around the buildings. There must have been a lookout of some kind, he decided.

Orl raced their vehicle down the creek bed until the animals were outdistanced, and then swung up one of the banks and through a narrow band of trees onto another small prairie. As they raced across the open ground, the vehicle which had been trailing them through the creek bed appeared behind them, and several more popped out of the trees to their right. This time Orl wasn't losing any ground; he held his lead easily and even increased it a bit when the pursuers fanned out behind them.

"Where are your magic hole-diggers?" Kari asked.

"It will take a separate stick for each car," Ross warned. "They aren't going to last long, at this rate."

"There is no need to use any, yet," Orl said. "I have the feeling that they will be more useful at a later time, and I believe we can lose pursuit in the forest ahead.'

Kari shrugged. "It seems foolish to leave behind live enemies who may cause more trouble later, but you are the chief magician."

"Everyone on the planet appears to be our enemy," Orl said. "We can't kill all of them."

"I suppose not," Kari agreed regretfully.

Orl did not slacken his speed in the slightest as the forest rushed at them, but shot the car between and around the trees with a skill that any racing driver on Earth would have envied. Ross felt less envy than he did stark terror, but while they repeatedly missed death by inches they never struck so much as a small branch.

Soon the pursuers were lost to sight entirely, but Orl continued his breakneck pace. Then, in the middle of a clump of larger trees that vaguely resembled weeping willows, the car stopped. A moment later it shot straight up at least a dozen feet, and then burrowed its way slowly among the leaves and branches. They were soon surrounded by a leafy screen, the ground invisible beneath them. Orl made another motion across the controls and the hissing of the machine died away to a whisper.

"This is it?" Ross asked incredulously. "We climb a tree and hope they go away?"

"It seems adequate," Orl said. "It requires a special operation to enable the vehicle to rise this high. I doubt that the barbarians know of it."

"You didn't think they knew how to drive across country, either," Ross reminded him, and then fell silent as one of the pursuing cars hissed by underneath them. Ross couldn't be sure, but he thought Orl looked smug as the other car shot by without pausing, and the noise faded into the distance.

"Incidentally," Ross said, "how come you know so much about these cars? I thought you were a newcomer to Venntra, too."

"These cars are the same type—perhaps the same cars—that were being produced at the time the Gates were closed. We preserved one of ours, and when our technology allowed us to do so, we built ours as nearly like it as we could. Elsprag lacks beam power, so ours are internally powered; otherwise they are the same. In any event, the operating controls are marked quite clearly; it is not difficult for anyone with mechanical training to follow them." He gestured at the blank control panel.

"That's another thing," Ross said. "The controls may be clearly marked to you, but some of us have a little difficulty in seeing them."

"Oh?" Orl cocked his head slightly to one side, like a bird inspecting a dubious worm. "You do not see these marked areas?"

"As far as I can tell," Ross assured him, "the entire panel is colored solid gray. No markings."

Orl looked at Kari. "Do you see anything?"

Kari peered closely at the blank panel. "It seems I am not trained in the proper spells," she admitted.

Orl was silent for a moment. "I can only think," he said finally, "that the spectrum to which humanoid eyes are sensitive is somewhat different from my own." He paused thoughtfully. "Perhaps that explains one thing Raka said, that rigorous training was required to learn to drive one of the vehicles. I assumed this was due to peculiarities of humanoid intelligence, but I can see that difficulties would arise if one could not see the controls."

"Quite a few of them," Ross agreed. Kari only nodded sagely, as if her theory of magic controls had been confirmed. Which in a way, Ross decided, it had.

"How long are we supposed to hide up here from those creatures?" Kari inquired. She included a strange word before "creatures"; Ross assumed it came from her native language and was derogatory. Now that he considered it, Venntran was remarkably deficient in terms of opprobrium. Not a good language for cursing, at all.

Orl motioned to the invisible controls, and the sounds of the forest became clearer. As far as Ross could tell, the windows were still closed, but the sounds came through as though they were open. Orl listened for a time and then did something to close off the sounds again. "It would appear to be safe at the present time," he said.

The hiss of the car returned to its normal volume, and Orl backed slowly out of the tree and settled down to the car's normal altitude of a foot or so.

"Where to now?" Ross asked.

"I am beginning to believe we should take a different approach," Orl said. "If you cannot see the controls, learning how to handle the vehicle would be considerably delayed. If necessary, we could try to disguise Kari and let her try to recover my equipment, but the barbarians will be more than usually alert, now that their city has disappeared."

The natives are restless, Ross thought, and then told his subconscious to go away until it could dredge up something useful.

"It might be more practical," Orl continued, "for us to conduct our investigation elsewhere, in some area in which the barbarians are not prevalent."

"You mean there are places like that? I sort of assumed they would spread all across the planet."

"Raka did not mention any widespread population, which leads me to believe that either they are congregated in a small area, bounded by our few Gates, or that they are in separate groups with little contact between such groups. A different tribe or clan might be easier to deal with, and at the very least would not be actively hunting us."

"Sounds good to me," Ross said. "I could do with less of this fleeing for my life, and more time to plan. Got any ideas of where to go?"

"From my map," Orl said, "there would seem to be another major city not far from here; certainly within a day's travel. Unless it has deteriorated far more than anything we have seen here, it should provide a source of information."

Ross settled back to watch the scenery as Orl drove. After only a few minutes, though, when the scenery proved monotonous, he found himself reflecting on the sheer insanity of his situation. Less than a day ago he was a cog in the great wheel of Earth industry, with a noisy if well-paying job running a bulldozer, and the imminent prospect of a less noisy and less well-paying job writing Commander Freff adventures. And now he was on a planet which even Commander Freff would scorn, hiding from barbarians who thought he had destroyed their city, and teamed up with an Amazon who could probably break him in half if he annoyed her and a talking dinosaur.

"Where did I go wrong?" he murmured to himself, and his treacherous subconscious replied, *by getting excited over an alien artifact instead of blowing it up like any right-thinking Earthman. Next time rely on dynamite and leave the investigating to the Commander.*

Thoughts of the valorous Commander brought an automatic response; *what would Commander Freff do in a situation like this? And why can't I do the same thing?*

The answer to the last question seemed painfully obvious; the Commander would take charge and solve everyone's problems, probably bringing civilization back to Venntra by the end of the book. And Ross couldn't do the same thing because he didn't have the Commander's advantages—or luck. Still, he had survived so far, which was no mean accomplishment, though there was no guarantee that he'd go on doing so.

"Come on Commander," he muttered to himself, "hang in there."

"What did you say?"

Ross jumped. For an instant, he thought that the Commander had answered him, but then he realized it was Kari.

"It's nothing," he said, a little sheepishly. "I was only talking to myself."

Kari stared at him, her eyes widening a trifle. "Talking to yourself? What do you tell yourself?"

"Nothing special. I just think out loud sometimes. Don't you ever do that?"

She frowned in puzzlement. "But what could I tell myself that I don't already know?"

It did sound a little strange when one put it that way, Ross realized. "It's just a habit. Sometimes it helps me to talk to myself, is all."

"Helps you do what?"

"Think." Kari opened her mouth to object, and Ross hastily tried to think of an example. "When I'm writing something, it helps me to. . . ." He realized there was no Venntran word for fiction, or plot outlines. "It helps me to make up stories," he finished, rather lamely.

"I do not understand. How can anyone make up stories? Stories describe what happened; you don't need to make them up."

"But sometimes I want to think about stories that didn't happen," Ross explained. There didn't seem to be a Venntran word for "imagination", either; this was getting difficult.

"But if something didn't happen, how can you think about it?"

Ross shook his head. This certainly was getting difficult. "Why, for example, what would have happened to Orl if you hadn't rescued him?"

"I don't know. I did rescue him."

"But if you hadn't, the barbarians would have probably killed him, right?"

Kari nodded. "But they didn't, so what good does it do you to make up stories about it?"

Ross sighed. "Just take my word for it. On Earth, it is very common; people spend a great deal of time thinking about things that never happened."

Kari looked incredulous. "It must be a very strange world."

"I suppose you're right. Anyway, my people are interested in things that never happened, and sometimes they pay people like me to make up stories, and when I'm doing it I sometimes think out loud. See?"

"No," Kari said. "You mean people give you food because you lie to them? I don't see why anyone would do that."

It was strange, Ross thought, that there was a Venntran word for "lie" but none for "imagination". A very practical race, evidently. "I suppose you could put it that way. But they all realize that what I write for them is not real." *Or at least, most of them do,* he amended silently to himself.

"But why would they want to know it, if it isn't real?" Kari persisted.

"Because they enjoy thinking about unreal things," Ross said. He was reminded of the time he had started a program to read the classics and decided it would definitely not be good policy to mention that some people read not-real things because it was supposed to be good for them.

Kari was apparently struggling with the concept that Ross's people enjoyed being lied to, and losing. "Do you ever tell stories about things that really happened?" she asked finally.

"Sometimes," Ross said, thinking back to a time when he had put in six months writing a maintenance and service manual for furnace dealers.

The frown had returned to Kari's face. "Was what you told us about yourself and Raka the truth?"

"Of course. I haven't lied to you at all. Anytime I make up a story for you, I'll tell you what I'm doing, okay? Besides, I do most of my lying in writing, not talking."

She shook her head. "You are a strange person, even

for a magician. If all the people on your world are like you, I don't think I would like your world. It would be too confusing."

"Well, it is, sometimes," Ross admitted. "But you'd probably get used to it."

"Maybe," she said doubtfully. "I suppose if you lie in writing, it wouldn't be so bad. I can't read, anyway."

Ross was momentarily startled, until he realized that there probably wasn't much in the way of a written language on Kari's world. "I could teach you," he offered.

"Why? So you can lie to me?"

Ross threw out his arms in despair. "Never mind. Tell me something about yourself." Anything to change the subject.

She studied him for a moment. "Do you want the truth? Or do you want me to lie?"

"The truth. Look, it is only under special conditions that lying is desirable, and I don't think those conditions exist here."

"Very well. I don't like all this talk of lying. I'm going to sleep."

"But we just slept," Ross protested, confused.

"Sleep when you have the chance," Kari informed him, not opening her eyes. "It prepares you for the times when you don't have the chance."

She was asleep almost before she finished talking. Ross envied her; none of this civilized business of having to "unwind" after a hard day's lying; just decide to go to sleep and do so. Relaxed, she looked less formidable. Her mouth had slipped into a half-smile, and except for a few minor details like facial coloring and that incredible hair she could have been one of the girls he knew on Earth. He wondered if she really would become accustomed to the use of imagination, as he'd assured her she would, or if this was something unique to Earth. Orl's race didn't seem overly imaginative, the barbarians here didn't really appear to be intelligent enough to have imaginations, and while Kari was intelligent enough she obviously knew nothing about the subject. *But surely*, he thought, *it must take some imagination to build any civilization? And Orl is civilized.*

After a time Ross took his eyes off Kari and looked at the terrain they were crossing. They had left the trees and were crossing another plain, much like the one they had been crossing yesterday when the terror had struck. Ross promptly tried to forget that incident, and failed; he suspected that he would never really forget it. Strange, though, that it hadn't bothered Kari so much, and apparently hadn't affected Orl at all. Was terror linked to the imaginative faculty of Earthmen?

As the featureless, yellow grass sped past, the feeling began to return, and momentarily Ross decided that imagination did have something to do with it; he imagined the terror and it appeared. But there had been no warning yesterday. He scanned the horizon and wondered if there really was something out there, watching him. A telepath, homing in on his mental faculties, ready to pounce. But the feeling built to a vague uneasiness and stayed that way, unlike yesterday's incredible fear.

Abruptly, the car stopped. Ross turned to look at Orl. The saurian's hands were drawn back from the control panel, his arms close to his body. His eyes seemed glazed as they darted glances in all direction.

"What's the matter?" Ross asked.

"I don't know! There is something. . . ." The words came sharply, harshly, and the rasping, grating sound of Orl's voice was stronger than ever, sounding as if the words were formed by scraping jagged stones together.

Ross reached forward to touch Orl reassuringly, but the saurian jerked backward violently, jamming himself against the side door. "I don't understand!" he grated. "There is nothing to be afraid of; it is not logical to be afraid of nothing!"

Kari had come awake as quickly as she had slept. "What is it?" she asked.

"I think it's the same thing that happened to us yesterday," Ross said, "only this time it's happening to Orl."

"But Orl is a great magician," she said. "He knows how to combat spells."

Ross shook his head. "Not this kind."

As Ross spoke, Orl's mouth opened, revealing the rows of serrated teeth in full. Ross had leaned forward to reassure him, but now leaned away again. If that mouth closed in panic, it could take an arm off. An unintelligible, scraping sound came from Orl's throat. Then one of his hands flew to the control panel, the car door vanished, and Orl was out of the car and stumbling across the plain.

"Come on," Ross said sharply, "we can't let him go like that."

Kari leaped from the car, temporarily abandoning her bow, and Ross scrambled out on her heels. Orl was running erratically, his arms flailing the air as if to ward off unseen blows, a hideous scraping wail sounding as though his throat was coming apart. Kari overtook him in seconds, and brought him crashing to the ground with a tackle that could have won her a place on the Miami Dolphins. As Ross arrived, she had maneuvered herself into a kneeling position on Orl's back, one hand pressing down on each of his arms. Orl's legs were still thrashing, and Ross fell on them and with some difficulty managed to pin them.

"Orl!" he shouted, trying to get the saurian's attention by sheer lung power. "Nothing is after you! It's all in your mind!"

It did no good. Orl had been absorbed by his own nightmares. Ross and Kari strained to hold him, as he struggled to escape from the terrors of his mind. It seemed hours that they remained in that position, Kari holding Orl's upper body while Ross strove to contain the legs, and to convince Orl—and just possibly himself —that there was nothing out there in the grass waiting to strike.

Eventually the thrashing grew less frantic, and the sound coming from Orl's throat lessened. When the struggling had subsided, Ross and Kari tentatively relaxed their holds, and when this produced no further outbursts, they stood up, watching Orl closely.

Slowly, the saurian rolled over on his side and lay there for a minute, motionless. Ross and Kari tensed to renew the combat if necessary. But whatever had attacked Orl was gone, back into whatever limbo it had come from. Orl's breathing was returning to normal, and his eyes had lost their glazed look. He stood up, staggering a bit, as though his ordeal had weakened him.

"It's over with?" Ross inquired.

Tentatively, Orl made his affirmative head-bobbing. "I assume," he said, "that this experience of mine was similar to the one you endured yesterday." He paused. "I found it—incredible. I have never even heard of such a thing among our race. It was not only the terror, though that was bad enough. In addition, I knew that the terror I was feeling was not logical. Not sane. Very rarely, we Elspragans become insane; it occurs often enough for us to know generally what the term means but not often enough for us to devote our still limited resources to a prolonged study of its causes. I felt, just a moment ago, as if I must be becoming insane; there seemed no other explanation." He chuckled, a bit weakly. "Being terrified of an invisible something out there in the grass is nothing compared to thinking that one is slipping into the ultimate horror of one's race."

Ross nodded understanding.

"Now it appears to be over," Orl continued. "I have control of my faculties; I can, from now on, only hope that I retain control of them. Another such ordeal might render me insane in truth. And from now on, every moment of the time I remain on Venntra, a little part of me will be waiting for the insanity to start." He stood silently for a moment. "I wonder," he said, "if this phenomenon had anything to do with the closing of the Gates?"

A shiver ran up Ross's spine. *Something* had caused the Gates to close, and something had either destroyed or driven out all of Orl's race who remained on Venntra after that closing. Repeated doses of that terror would do it—but how? Could terror be communicated like a disease? Or perhaps by a disease? That was an idea, although he couldn't imagine what sort of disease it would be that would produce similar symptoms in himself, Kari, and Orl.

"Now we have more reason than ever to continue to the other city and seek information," Orl said. He seemed to have recovered from his ordeal, and led the way as they tramped back to the car.

After a few miles, a Venntran road cut across their path and Orl turned the car onto it, speeding up to take advantage of the flat surface. Kari had returned to her interrupted sleep, and Ross was trying to sort out things in his mind. None of the ideas he came up with could survive the barest scrutiny. If the fits of terror were caused by something in the air, then why had it affected them at different times? Or why had it affected all three of them at all? He and Kari might have considerable biological similarity, but the only thing they had in common with Orl was that they were all oxygen breathers.

Sound waves? Subsonics? He recalled reading that certain frequencies below the threshold of human hearing could cause unreasoning terror. But could those frequencies be projected on an open prairie? And would they affect a medium-size dinosaur? Maybe, but. . . .

He wondered if Orl had been right in his speculation that the fits of terror had something to do with the closing of the Gates and the destruction of Venntran civilization. He could imagine that if they covered the planet, and lasted long enough, they could do the job. But surely if that had been the case, one of the Venntran scientists would have found a cure for them before everything was smashed.

But if the effect had smashed Venntran civilization, why was it operating on such a spotty basis now? It didn't seem to be bothering the barbarians. Ross's head whirled. This was the trouble of being on the wrong end of the typewriter. Commander Freff could speculate like this for a few minutes and come up with the right answer, because Ross knew the right answer all along. It was terribly frustrating to be unable to come up with an answer at all.

Giving up his speculations, Ross took an interest in the landscape again. Ahead lay a range of mountains, perhaps the same ones he had noticed yesterday. He tried to remember the direction they had been traveling and any distinctive shapes of the peaks, but couldn't. The grass had changed from sickly yellow to pale green and it was thinning out. Here and there, startlingly blue flowers poked out above the level of the grass. An occasional grove of trees stood out, trees with strangely pointed tops, like huge dunce caps, perched on top of irregular, cylindrical trunks.

As Ross watched a single tree approach on the right side of the road, the car began to slow. He glanced questioningly at Orl. The saurian made a motion across the control panel, and the car began to pick up speed again.

But only for a moment. Again it began to slow.

Again Orl passed a hand over the control panel, and for a moment the speed seemed to increase. Again it slowed, and continued to slow.

"Something wrong?" Ross asked, thinking immediately that it was a dumb question; obviously something was wrong. "I mean, do you know what's wrong?"

"I don't know," Orl said, passing his hand again across the control panel. This time there was no response at all, and the car came to a full stop. "The vehicle no longer answers the controls."

"Could the power be off? Maybe we're outside the range of the power beam."

"No, the engine is still running," Orl said. "Unless there has been a mammoth failure of components, the power beams covered the planet. However, the vehicle will not move forward. It does not seem logical."

"Like everything else on this planet," Ross commented.

CHAPTER 6

Orl glanced at Ross briefly, but immediately returned his attention to the vehicle's controls. He made more gestures across the surface of the panel, touching it lightly several times. Ross thought he could feel a faint vibration beneath his feet, but that was all.

Kari was awake by now, looking around curiously. "Why are we stopped?" she asked.

"We're stuck," Ross said. "I'm not sure what we're stuck in, though."

Kari looked at him skeptically. "The truth?"

"The truth," Ross said, resisting an impulse to add "cross my heart and hope to die," and realizing that perhaps he had made a mistake in trying to explain to her about fiction.

Orl made more gestures, and the vehicle began moving slowly backward. After backing for several yards, Orl swung the car off the road and took it a hundred yards or more before turning parallel to the road and starting it forward again.

Again the car stopped, no farther forward than it had been on the road.

"Strange," Orl said, finally. "There is a barrier of some form which is stopping our forward progress."

"A force field?" Ross asked.

Orl glanced at him but said nothing; apparently the situation was too serious for amusement at inferior scientific concepts. Again Orl backed the car away from whatever it was that was stopping them, and drove across country, this time for at least a half-mile, before turning and starting forward parallel to the road.

Again they came to a slow stop after a dozen or more yards.

"I don't see anything," Kari announced. "This is more magic?"

"Something like that," Ross agreed. "And this time it looks like it's bigger magic than we can handle."

"I'm beginning to dislike Venntra," Kari said. "Too much magic; nothing you can sink your knife into." She was silent for a moment, watching Orl trying vainly to coax the vehicle forward. "Would it help if we got out and pushed?" she asked.

Ross started to laugh, but then he saw that Orl was treating the question seriously.

"It seems unlikely that human muscles can prevail where the vehicle fails," Orl said. "But it is a different form of power. If this force is a modification of the power beam, it would not operate on muscle power. I believe it is worth attempting; the effort may provide information even if it does not succeed."

Kari was looking rather baffled, so Ross interpreted. "He said yes."

A moment later, the side panels of the car vanished, and Ross realized instantly that pushing would do them no good. Suddenly, he felt as though he was submerged in thick, transparent jelly. He could barely move. Kari, who had been moving toward the opening, seemed to be in slow motion. The only sudden change of any kind was the expression of total puzzlement which appeared on her face.

"What is happening? I cannot move!" Her voice was no longer baritone but a rich bass. The words came out at their regular pace, but the tone was an octave deeper than normal. Even so, terror was evident.

Orl's hands were moving across the control panel, now with agonizing slowness.

"The doors," he said after nearly a minute of slow hand motions, "will not close. Nothing will work." His voice, instead of sounding like grating rocks, now sounded like colliding, cracking boulders.

"We can't even back out?" Ross's own voice startled him with its incredible deepness.

"It appears not. The controls have no effect."

A sinking feeling assaulted Ross's stomach. To be stranded on a strange world was bad enough, but to be trapped like a fly in amber. . . .

Then there was something else, a faint tingling sensation, then a growing numbness, first in his toes, then moving slowing into the rest of his feet.

"Come on!" he gave a rumbling shout. "We have to get out of here; it's starting to affect our bodies!"

Still in slow motion, Kari grasped her bow while Ross picked up the briefcase containing the remaining dynamite and the food packets. If they had to abandon the car, they would need the food more than ever. Kari was moving out of the door, and Ross could see that even gravity appeared to be affected. It was a full two seconds from the time Kari stepped from the car until she touched the ground barely two feet below.

Ross and Orl floated to the ground on opposite sides of the car. Ross was beginning to wonder if at this speed they could get out of the field before the numbness spread far enough through their bodies to prevent any movement at all. His muscles straining, he tried to lunge forward as he finally hit the ground, but his body only tilted forward with agonizing slowness, and his legs, ordered to run, would only move slowly and with much effort. He imagined they all three must look like athletes seen in a slow-motion film. First one foot touched the ground. Ross could feel the impact, even through the numbness, as his shoe dug into the dirt, and he could see the ground move slowly beneath him as the leg straightened, forcing him forward. Then the other foot dug in, and that leg straightened. Now his body seemed to be nearly horizontal, yet he didn't fall. The briefcase, still gripped tightly in one hand as his arms swung in a slow-motion parody of their normal motion, felt like a lead weight on the end of a yard-long pendulum.

Now the first leg again, digging in, forcing him forward again, and now the other, slowly, slowly forcing him forward. Already his lungs were struggling for air; was it his imagination, or was the air itself actually thicker and harder to breathe? Or was the numbness beginning to reach his lungs and slow them down?

He could hear his heart pounding, not at the rapid, rattling rate that it should have been, but slowly, like a huge pulsing balloon being stretched beyond its limits again and again, straining to force the thickening jelly of his blood through his veins.

Feeling had gone from his lower body. Were his legs still moving? He couldn't tell. Vision was beginning to dim. His last sight was going to be the yellowish grass of an alien world.

Then there was a hand grasping his, pulling him forward, and suddenly the pressure was gone and he was sprawled on his face in the grass. The air was breathable, his heart was racing at a speed normal for the exertion he had subjected it to, and he could feel the grass between the fingers of his left hand and the handle of the briefcase in his right.

It was wonderful just to lie there in the nice, normal alien air, but something was prodding him in the ribs, and Kari's voice, back to its normal baritone, was insisting that he get up.

"Come on! We've got to help Orl!"

Ross struggled to his feet. Every muscle protested, but he made it.

Orl lay less than ten feet away, both arms stretched out in front of him. Ross could see his chest laboring to breathe.

Ross's entire being rebelled at the thought of walking back into that force field or whatever it was, and he looked around desperately for an alternative. His eye fell on Kari's six-foot longbow. Picking it up, he walked cautiously forward until he felt the air becoming thick in front of him, and extended the bow toward Orl.

It didn't reach. Ross had a strong desire to abandon his attempt, but Orl and Kari were both watching him now, so he was stuck with the logical conclusion. *Besides*, he thought, *what would Commander Freff say if his creator failed a little test of nerve like this?* Suddenly realizing what he had been thinking, he decided that since Commander Freff's creator was obviously going bananas, he might as well get it over with.

"Hang onto my ankles," he told Kari.

She got a good grip, and Ross forced himself to fall forward, into the force field.

His fall through the thickening air seemed incredibly prolonged, but he still felt the jar when he landed, taking most of the force on his left hand to protect the bow. Lying there, with lungs laboring and his heart beginning that slow, ballooning pulsing again, he forced the bow out before him, toward Orl's fingers. *If he isn't too paralyzed to grab it,* he thought.

Orl wasn't. When the bow touched his fingers, they began slowly to close over it. Ross waited until they had what seemed to be a solid grip, and then tried to crawl backwards. He couldn't do it. No matter how he strained, Orl's weight on the other end of the bow anchored him solidly to the ground. Then there was pressure on his ankles, and he began sliding backwards, ever so slowly, across grass which he could no longer feel. The curve of the bow straightened, and then Orl was slowly sliding forward and Ross felt as if he was slowly being pulled apart. He could hear Kari as she grunted and strained behind him, and he pushed against the ground with his numb left hand, less in an attempt to be helpful than in desperation to relieve the agonizing pull on his ankles. But he hung onto the bow.

Then his body was out of the field, and he could sit up, brace his legs and heave, while Kari was beside him, reaching for the bow. Orl came sliding out of the field, relaxing his hold on the bow and sprawling limply on the ground. Ross sat beside him, trying to gather a little strength before making the supreme effort of standing up.

Kari was breathing hard, and beads of perspiration stood out like crystals against the black skin. She was standing, however, and after a short time began pacing back and forth. Picking up something from the ground, she turned in the direction of the car, drew back her arm, and threw with all her strength.

The object sailed through the air, but then slowed down as it reached the force field boundary, and Ross saw it was a small stone. It did not fall, but continued to move forward at a reduced speed, only gradually beginning to arc downward. It took several seconds for it to fall to the ground, and then it landed several feet short of the car.

Ross thought once again of Clarke's third law, about the indistinguishability of magic and advanced science. To Kari, this was pure magic. To himself, it was advanced science—but in the end, it amounted to the same thing. The only thing that mattered now was to discover who the magician was and what he was trying to do. *Or what she is trying to do, or what it is trying to do*, his conscience reminded him. *Don't be chauvinistic.*

They weren't going to find out the answers by sitting here, obviously. With his muscles protesting, Ross got up, staggered for a moment, and took a few tentative steps to make sure that he still could. The car, he noticed, was settling slowly to the ground. The grass beneath it was already bending beneath its weight, and he could see the faint motion of its descent. There was no sound; not even the usual hissing. Orl was still sprawled where he and Kari had dragged him, and Ross went over to look down at him. If anything happened to Orl, there went his chances of getting out of this crazy place.

"He's breathing normally," Kari said. "He'll be all right."

"You seem awfully sure," Ross commented.

"I've seen a lot of injured, dying, and dead humans and animals of all sorts. Orl isn't one of them. He was in the magic place longer than we were, so it will take him longer to recover, that's all."

He was there longer, his metabolism is completely different, and it may not have affected him the same way it did us, Ross thought, but he didn't voice the thought. *If you can't help, don't worry*, was one of the Commander's maxims.

102

"If he does recover, he'll owe you his life," he told Kari. "I already do. Are all the women on your planet that, uh, powerful? I thought you were going to pull my ankles off, and if it got me out of that force field I didn't much care."

Kari grinned at him. "I was always considered strong," she said. "The young men in my village were afraid of me. Especially after I killed one for trying to make love to me."

"Yeah, that would be sort of discouraging," Ross admitted. "You have rules about lovemaking on your world, then?"

"No. Why should we have rules? It's a natural thing for men and women to do. But this time my head hurt, and I didn't feel like it, and he insisted."

"So you killed him for it?"

"I hit him harder than I intended to," she explained. "With a rock. Anyway, nobody from my village was much loss. The nomads were better, but I didn't really like them much, either. The people here aren't any better than the ones on Leean, but I guess," she added thoughtfully, "that you and Orl are all right. I never knew any magicians before; we didn't have many on Leean."

Leean, Ross decided, must be a squalid little planet. He was about to ask more about it when a rumble from Orl diverted his attention. The saurian was sitting up, holding his head in his hands and obviously feeling terrible. Ross grinned sympathetically; he well knew that feeling.

"You seem to be improving, anyway," he remarked. "Kari said you'd be all right, but I was a bit worried. Among other things, we need you."

Orl muttered something unintelligible.

"How come you were by yourself, anyway?" Ross

asked, struck by something that had been subconsciously bothering him. "On Solthree, or Earth"—he used the English "Earth" in place of the Venntran one—we almost never send one lone scientist out to solve a problem. We use teams."

Still holding his head, Orl replied, "We are also generally organized into teams on Elsprag. But this was considered a very dangerous operation; we could not afford to risk a great amount of manpower, or any scientists at all. We need our scientists to solve problems at home."

Ross was momentarily stunned. "But," he said, "I thought you were a scientist."

Orl waved a hand in the air, and after a moment Ross realized that he was asking to be helped to his feet. With Kari helping, they got the saurian upright, and he shuffled in a small circle on the grass, stumbling now and then.

"No," he said. "I am not a scientist at all, though I have had enough training to be able to recognize the machinery and the aura of the old Venntrans. Basically, I am a seeker and a communicator."

Ross got nothing out of the word "aura"; it seemed to have something to do with mental emanations, but a mental emanation which might be left behind in a deserted city, like a broken tool. "Seeker" seemed to cover pretty much what the English word "explorer" did, in its widest application, such as exploring new fields of knowledge. It also had a concept of thinking strange and unreal thoughts. Orl, then, was more imaginative than most of his race, which was a startling idea. But it was the last word that brought Ross up with a jolt.

"Then I was right," he said. "You're a mind reader!"

Orl rotated his head negatively. "Not minds; not even of my own race. I can sense attitudes, you might say. I can tell when someone means harm to me, when he is telling the truth and when he is not; other things of that nature. Coupled with an analysis of alternatives, I can sometimes predict what an individual will do next, though since attitudes are constantly changing, it is impossible to extend this talent very far into the future."

"Then that's where you got the idea that I'd be useful to you when you'd just met me."

"Not precisely. Being able to foretell the usefulness of any individual is a separate talent, which few Elspragans possess. Therefore I was considered ideal for the purpose of returning to Venntra. I would not need companions; I could recruit trustworthy allies after I went through the Gate."

"Trustworthy, maybe, but not all that useful so far," Ross commented. "Any ideas on getting the car back?"

"None that I know of. We cannot reach it, and even if we could, I believe that its engine was ruined when the doors were opened. That was my fault. I should have realized that the field generated by the vehicle itself would operate to some extent to nullify the barrier field, and that opening the doors would create a break in that field."

"They're the same force, then?"

"It is quite possible that they are the same type of force, used for different purposes. I have never encountered it projected as a barrier, however. They may be entirely different."

Ross shrugged. "So we walk."

"It would seem to be our only choice."

So walk they did, back toward the remnants of the city and the Temple where Orl's instruments might or might not be kept, and might or might not be accessible to them. The first hour was almost pleasant for Ross, who had always enjoyed getting out into the country and seldom had a chance to do so on Earth. Getting a close look at the trees and grass reminded him of the sheer wonder of his being on an alien planet. He tried to converse with Orl, but the big saurian was obviously not used to much walking and had to keep his attention on putting his feet down without stumbling over anything. Kari tended to outdistance them every few minutes and then stand impatiently waiting for them.

The second hour was not bad, nor was the third, though by that time Ross was beginning to emulate Orl and put his full attention on where his feet were going. By the fourth hour, despite rest stops, Ross's muscles were protesting violently.

By the fifth hour, every muscle from the waist down was wailing in agony. The worst seemed to be his shins, which felt as if someone had been pounding on them with a hammer. Each time he brought his foot down, a new blow was struck. It was getting impossible to lift his feet more than an inch or so above the ground, so he moved in a jerky shuffle. If they spotted a carload of barbarians coming down the road, he was not sure that he would be able to negotiate the high grass alongside the road.

Orl, from his slowed pace and delicate movements, seemed to be faring no better; probably worse. Only Kari seemed untouched. Her movements were as free and full after five hours as they had been at the start, and Ross was beginning to hate her. Her waits for them to catch up had grown steadily longer.

Ross wondered how a simple thing like walking could do this to him. He had done plenty of walking on Earth.

In the last few years, he'd even taken up jogging, sometimes as much as three miles at a time. Could this be the alien environment, or what?

In the end, though the sun was still high in the sky and Kari impatient to be going, they stopped. Ross and Orl struggled through the grass to a stand of trees not far from the road.

After they had been still long enough for some of the pain to subside, Ross began to speculate on what was causing their problems on Venntra. Orl simply looked uncomprehending as the beginning, while Kari had her stock answer.

"Magic, of course."

"Yes, but what kind of magic? And who's the magician?"

Kari shrugged, an act she had begun to copy from Ross. "That's for other magicians to find out."

"All right; that's what I'm trying to do. But all I can come up with is that there is an invisible Menace out there specifically assigned to the job of frustrating whatever we do, and I don't really believe that myself. Much."

Nobody bothered to comment, and Ross scanned mentally through several hundred science fictional gimmicks for one that might fit. "How about somebody that wants to keep us penned up, like domestic animals?" he suggested. "The force field barrier is just the fence that keeps us and the barbarians restricted to this area. That's why Raka didn't know anything about the rest of the planet."

"Why?" Orl inquired.

"Why what?" Ross answered, a trifle confused.

"Why would anyone want to restrict our movements?"

107

"How should I know? You're the expert on aliens. A scientific exercise of some kind. Sociological, ecological —how long it takes a given number of humanoids to wipe out all life including themselves in an area of pre-determined size. Our scientists are always running experiments like that."

Kari snorted in contempt, while Orl looked puzzled. "Why should anyone want to know that?" he inquired.

"*I* don't know! I never participated. But experiments were made. Mostly with small animals, but then maybe our experimenter is so different from us that he considers us small and unintelligent."

"If that's the sort of world Earth is," Kari said, "I'm surprised you want to go back."

This time Ross snorted, and went back to thinking. After a while, he tried again. "Look. It's been two hundred of your generations since the Gates were closed. I don't know how long that is in Earth years—we'll have to compare notes on time eventually—but it's a good long period. You said earlier that some of the equipment left behind might have been damaged."

"But none of it has been," Orl pointed out. "Some of it is doing things that aren't even in our records."

"That's what I mean. Now, you said this computer used to run everything on Venntra, right?"

"Yes, but I don't quite see. . . ."

"And you said that insanity was rare on Elsprag but it did occur."

Orl suddenly understood the nature of Ross's conjecture. "And you believe the Venntran computer has gone insane? But insanity is a defect in thought, and in value considerations. The computer neither thinks nor has an independent value system."

"You mean it didn't have when your ancestors left.

108

But that wasn't quite what I meant, anyway. We've got computers on Earth, though none as complicated as this one. And sometimes they go haywire. It isn't technically insanity; it's an imperfect resistor or a circuit failure or some flaw in mechanical design—but it produces results that don't make sense. If your computer is more complicated and more powerful, it could produce more complicated and powerful mistakes."

Orl circled his head in assent. "An ingenious theory. It would explain why we can detect no pattern in the events here; the computer is, at least part of the time, producing illogical responses to its input. But the most pervasive activity of the computer, now that it is not providing for a civilization, is the maintenance of the power beams. It seems odd that a random response would not affect them at some time."

"Maybe it has, and we weren't in a position to notice it."

The discussion continued, but as Ross realized, the speculation was fruitless. Even if he was right, how do you outguess a faulty computer? And he had no proof that he was correct. Maybe Kari had the right idea; put it all down to magic and quit worrying about it. Except that wouldn't get them any answers, and answers were what they needed to get them off this planet.

Kari had given up and gone to sleep in the middle of the discussion. As the voices ceased, she came awake, announcing that from now on one of them had better stand guard, and she'd watch while Ross and Orl slept.

When Ross awoke, it was night, and he rolled over where he lay and looked hopefully at the stars. He wasn't sure what he was looking for. A familiar constellation, even if he could recognize it, would tell him little. It might mean that he was only a few light years from Earth instead of a million, but that made little difference. Without the Gates operating, the next solar system was as remote as the next galaxy. Yet he was disappointed when he could find nothing familiar. There was a broad band across the sky, similar to the Milky Way, but at one point there was a mass of brightness, stars by the millions it seemed, that was like nothing seen from Earth. It covered two or three degrees of the sky, and its brightness was equal to that of a half-moon back on Earth. There appeared to be no moon here to dispute its dominance of the heavens.

He wondered if it was the center of the galaxy, viewed from some point far closer to it than Earth was. For a moment, the sense of anticipation which he had felt a number of times yesterday plucked again at the edge of his mind. The center of the galaxy! Or could it be the center of another galaxy? No point in restricting his dreams to one paltry galaxy.

However, the mood didn't hold. As he lay there, the alient sky stretching above him, his body still aching from strains of the day, a sense of loss began to well up within him. The fact that he was on an alien planet, that ships had indeed traveled from star to star and even, at some time deep in the past, to Earth itself, did nothing to cheer him. The only thought that gave the slightest reassurance was the possibility that they could find the Gate to Earth and be able to reopen it. He was thinking about that when he drifted off to sleep again.

Ross's dreams were of Earth. They were not, however, pleasant dreams. More than once he awakened to find himself shaking uncontrollably, screaming silently in his mind. All the dreams centered on the few days more than fifteen years before, when he and his father had camped out in one of the national parks. Nothing had happened at the time, but now, in his dream recollections of the event, everything happened. Each unidentified sound in the night became a real and terrifying animal, stalking him relentlessly. A dozen times that night, he had scrambled from his sleeping bag and run, terrified, into the darkness. Behind him, he would hear the padding feet, the crackling of branches, the snarl or growl or bellow of whatever animal was pursuing him. And then the silence, as his pursuer left the ground in a final leap and he waited for its impact on his back.

Each time, he would awaken to the alien skies of Venntra, and for an irrational moment wish he were back in the nightmarish dream world, if only so that he could die on Earth and not here on an insane alien world.

Once he awakened to find Kari leaning over him, looking worried. He tried to explain that he had been having a bad dream, but he couldn't. In the Venntran language there seemed to be no word for dream. In the end, he had to explain dreams in the same terms he had used for imagination.

Kari looked incredulous. "You mean that when you sleep, you lie even to yourself?"

"Something like that," he admitted.

"I do not understand."

"Well, I don't either, really. Neither do any of the magicians on Earth. They have studied this for many years, but they don't really know what causes it. All they know is that it is necessary. Unless we lie to ourselves in sleep, our minds grow sick."

Kari shook her head in the darkness. "Your people are strange, Rossallen. Perhaps it is because they are a race of magicians. They have become infected by the strange things they study."

111

CHAPTER 7

Ross grinned in the darkness. "Better watch out; I might infect you."

She snorted. "Your people read too many lies. As long as I can't read I'll be able to tell what's real and what isn't."

That last statement was debatable, Ross decided, but the first one was right on target. "Doesn't anyone read on Leean?" he asked. "You know the word."

"Some people do. The merchants must keep records, some of the cities have kings who record great events, there are a few books about magic. I've never needed to. The dangers on Leean are those that can be seen and heard and fought. They aren't invisible and treacherous as they are here."

"Tell me about Leean," Ross suggested.

She looked at him oddly. "The truth?" she asked.

"The truth."

"What do you want to know?" She sounded a bit uncertain, and Ross was silent for a moment. He has asked what could be a tough question for someone who had just realized a few days ago that more than one world existed. If someone had asked him to tell them all about Earth, where would he have started?

"Start with yourself," he said finally. "Were you a warrior, a fighter?"

"No more than necessary," she said. "I have always wanted to be able to take care of myself. That's why this world frightens me; I don't know how to fight magic."

"You said you didn't think very highly of the people in your village; why?"

"Because they are stupid grubbers in the dirt, who don't know anything that happens beyond the border of the village lands, and don't want to know." Kari continued to explain her distaste for village life at some length. She remembered her first job, as a little girl, was weeding the crops; she'd done that almost as soon as she could walk. There had been other duties, all of them distasteful. She had wanted to be a tomboy and never been allowed to be; Ross gathered that the division between men's and women's activities was even sharper on Leean than it was in primitive societies on Earth.

"Then when I was older the dry times came," she said. A desert area had encroached on the village, until eventually the villagers had moved to new land, taking it from another village. The fighting had decimated both villages, until in the end the survivors had banded together and shared the increasingly sterile land.

"I was good at the fighting," Kari said, a trifle smugly. "Since our village lost a lot of its men, I was allowed to carry a bow and a knife. They wouldn't let me lead the men into battle, though; they said it wasn't right for a woman. I could have won that war. . . ." She broke off. "Anyway, after the fighting I was expected to settle down, take a husband, and go back to a woman's duties. But by then all the men were afraid of me. Most of them had been even before the fighting, but I told you about killing that man."

"I can't say I blame the men," Ross commented. "You don't sound like the ideal wife."

Kari laughed. "That's what I told that nomad, but he didn't believe me." After she had reached her full growth, a band of nomads had ridden through the

113

village. A dozen villagers had been slaughtered, and food, weapons, and half a dozen younger women were taken.

Kari had gone along without too much protest. "By that time, I knew that I didn't want to live the rest of my life in that village. But that night when the nomad came to me, I told him I didn't want to spend the rest of my life with him, either. In the end I had to kill him with his own knife in order to get away."

After that, she had become a solitary wanderer over Leean, looking for a place or a person she could be satisfied with. Occasionally she stopped in drought-stricken villages and worked for her meals, occasionally she had raided nomad camps for supplies. But mostly she hunted, until she felt sure that her skill with bow, knife and spear was the equal of that of anyone on Leean. Occasionally, she'd had to prove that it was.

Then she had discovered what had seemed to be a cave, half-hidden behind a pile of rocks in a barren valley. Curious, she had gone inside—and found herself on Venntra. She had mixed feelings about Venntra. Life was easier here than it had been on Leean, but the presence of so much magic disturbed her.

"Now your turn," she said. "Tell me about your magician's planet."

Ross had felt that as a writer he understood Earth-type humanity pretty well. By the time he had explained to Kari's satisfaction what an education was, what basketball was, why anyone would provide him with an education in return for his playing basketball, what New York was like, why anyone would live there, what money was, why he was paid money for driving a bull-dozer, what a housing development was and why anyone would live there, he realized that his understanding was considerably more superficial than he had thought it was.

In the end, she returned to the dreams, which she was totally unable to comprehend, finally deciding that magicians were strange people and, except possibly for Ross, not worth associating with.

Ross wondered about the lack of a word for either dreams or imagination in the Venntran vocabulary. Were these things unique to Earth? And if so, why? After Kari had left and he was slowly returning to sleep, the question lingered in his mind, inspiring dreams of its own.

The first thing Ross noticed in the morning was that he could stand up and walk. After the previous day, he hadn't been positive that he could. The process was still painful, but after a few minutes it became bearable and didn't seem to get worse as time went on. Even Orl seemed partially recovered. Their progress, however, was slow compared to the first hours of the day before.

When they stopped for lunch, and Ross was pulling some of their dwindling supply of food from the briefcase, Kari reached in and picked up a stick of dynamite.

"Careful with that," Ross advised. He had started to remove the caps and fuse during one of their rest periods the day before, but decided that he wasn't sure he could do it without setting the whole thing off, so had left the cap in place and handled the briefcase gingerly.

"How does this magic work?" Kari asked.

Ross shrugged. Why not teach her? "Let me have it a minute, and I'll show you," he said.

She gave it back to him, and Ross sighed with relief. "You have to set fire to this part," he said, showing her the fuse, "and then get away from it as far as you can." He explained the difficulty in timing it, and she looked at him oddly.

"Give me a piece of that part you set fire to," she said, "and show me how you do it."

Using Kari's knife, he cut a three-inch length from the end of the fuse, then got the lighter out of the other compartment of the briefcase. By calling the lighter an improved form of flint and steel and ignoring the fuel, he managed to get that explained in a few minutes, and lit the fuse. Kari watched it closely as it burned and moved her head slightly at regular intervals. After it had burned out, she nodded.

"I see it now," she said.

Ross felt a bit sheepish. Timing the fuse by burning a test length was a perfectly obvious thing to do, which he should have thought of. He put himself back on firm ground by explaining that with the cap in place, a fuse wasn't always necessary. Sometimes the dynamite would go off if you dropped it, and it was wise to be very careful.

"Why don't you take the caps off, then?" she asked.

Ross grimaced. "Because I'm afraid to; they might explode while I was trying to remove them. I'm not really an expert on this stuff."

Kari nodded solemnly and watched Ross replace the dynamite in the briefcase.

During the afternoon march, Ross remembered to ask Orl about dreams. Orl, like Kari, failed to comprehend. Sleep was a time when all activity ceased; both mind and body rested. Dreams, it seemed to him, defeated the purpose of sleep.

They also discussed time scales briefly, eventually deciding that the two hundred generations that had elapsed from the closing of the Gates until the present was at least 12,000 Earth years. If they had done all their conversions correctly, at least; figured in Earth generations it would be closer to 60,000 years, and from exchanges of personal ages Orl didn't seem to be all that much shorter-lived than humans. A good long while, anyway. Ross wondered if a group of two or three hundred humans with the equivalent recorded knowledge would take that long to build their civilization back to Elsprag's present level. On Earth, a somewhat larger group had gone from planting sticks and stone knives to combine harvesters and computers in that time length or less, and invented all their concepts as they went. Did the lack of imagination have any bearing? Where would Earth be without imagination? Still plodding along somewhere in the early iron age?

On the other hand, Ross considered the hundreds of irrational, insane acts recorded in Earth newspapers every day. Perhaps the slow, plodding, logical way was the only way to reach truly great heights. Earth had come a long way in a short time, compared to Elsprag, but Elsprag would, eventually, recover all the knowledge of its Venntran parent. Would Earth ever get that far, or would it destroy itself first?

Ross temporarily lost interest in the comparative value of logic and imagination that evening. The animal was in the distance, at least a half mile away across one of the little plains of Venntra. The Venntran sun was just below the horizon, but Ross was still positive of his identification. He had seen reconstructions of it in museums, and imitations of it running through countless movies lost continents and prehistoric tribes.

It was a mammoth, huge and hairy, larger than an elephant, its tusks nearly as long as its trunk, curling around in front of the body. It lumbered across an open area between two stands of trees and was gone. It made no sound.

"Did you see that?" Ross said.

"The big shaggy thing?" Kari asked. "Yes, I saw it. Why?"

"That was an animal that has been extinct on Earth for thousands of years. What's it doing here?"

If a bulldozer can come through the Gate in the 1970s, why couldn't a few mammoths come through a few thousands of years earlier? he mentally questioned himself. *Don't be a dummy.*

Orl looked questioning, so Ross explained. "But I wonder," he went on after a moment, how many other animals came through? Or could it be that only large ones are heavy enough to trigger the Gate?"

"Perhaps," Orl said, not showing any great interest. "But didn't you say your companion came through it after you? How heavy was he?"

"Shot down again," Ross muttered. This sort of thing never happened to Commander Freff.

That night it seemed that nearly every Earth animal that had ever existed must have come through the Gate. Ross could place the coughing roar of a lion, which he had heard on a TV show, and the howl of a timber wolf, which he had heard in person some years ago. There were a thousand others, almost continuous, completely unidentifiable. More than once he thought of awakening the others and suggesting they move on, but where could they go? They needed to locate another Gate building. Or another car. However, they saw nothing more. There were only the sounds. During his turn to sleep, Ross shut them out of his mind. His sleep was interrupted only by a continuation of the same dreams he had suffered through the night before. Once he must have cried out, for he woke up to find Kari firmly shushing him with a hand over his mouth. The hand was still there when he went back to sleep.

The sky was already light when Ross opened his eyes. Kari was asleep nearby, while a crackling in a nearby bush might be an elephant about to attack but was more likely Orl trying to be quiet. For some reason Ross felt better this morning. They were about out of food, but now that large animals had begun to appear they could probably live by hunting. Kari could certainly kill game, and Ross might be able to help somewhat. Between them they should be able to provide for Orl. At the thought of Orl's helplessness in the outdoors, he chuckled at bit. If this was an Elspragan explorer, what were the rest of his race like?

Then, as he was sitting up, he saw it.

It looked like a wolf, but it stood over four feet high at the shoulder and its grizzled, brownish grey head was larger than Ross's own. It stood next to a tree less than fifty feet away, staring at them. Ross froze in a half-sitting position. How long would it take him to dig the gun from its pouch, get it pointed in the right direction, and squeeze the reluctant trigger?

Too long, probably, if it decided to charge. Better not make any sudden moves, and hope Orl quits bumbling around there in the bushes. Of course, the reputation of wolves for viciousness was totally undeserved; they didn't attack humans. But ordinary wolves didn't grow to the size of this thing.

Suddenly he recognized it. A dire wolf. He remembered a picture; a reconstruction. The animal, like the mammoth, was extinct, but bones had been found somewhere. Which meant that it probably wouldn't even know what a human was, and could just as well think they were its breakfast.

As he recognized it, it came alive. Its eyes glittered in the early morning light, the jaws moved menacingly, and it charged.

Frantically, Ross tried to drag the gun from the pouch that still hung from his waist, and as he did there was a blur of motion on his left. Kari had evidently waked up sometime during Ross's contemplation of the beast, and was now snatching up her bow. As Ross got the pistol out, Kari slipped her bowstring into place in one smooth motion, notched an arrow, and fired from a crouch.

The arrow struck the wolf in the shoulder, and apparently did nothing but annoy it. Then Ross had the pistol out and swung it up as the beast leaped for him. As in his nightmares, he wasn't fast enough; the animal slashed at his extended arm, and he dropped the pistol.

Before the wolf's jaws could close on him a second time another arrow sprouted from its neck, and it turned and lunged for Kari, who was now erect and fitting a third arrow to the bow. Moving faster than he thought possible, Ross scooped up the gun with his left hand and fired awkwardly. There was a crackling sound and the grass a foot behind the creature vanished. Holding the trigger down, he swung the gun, bringing his injured right arm around to help steady it. As the wolf crouched to spring at Kari, Ross's shot caught it in the back legs. The lower part of the legs disappeared and the animal sprawled forward instead of leaping, the claws of its front feet raking at Kari's legs. Kari had dropped her bow and snatched out her knife as the beast crouched; now she backed away warily. The wolf followed her, pulling itself along on its front legs.

Ross aimed as carefully as he could, steadying the pistol with both hands despite the agony in his right arm. When he fired, the upper part of the animal's head disappeared, and it abruptly collapsed. With a conscious effort, Ross unclamped his fingers from the gun and released the trigger. His right arm fell to his side limply.

A sound behind him caused him to whirl around, but it was only Orl plunging through the bushes.

"What happened?" Orl demanded. "What is that creature?"

Ross got to his feet and walked cautiously toward the fallen wolf. "That's a good question," he said. "As near as I can tell, it's another Earth creature, now extinct on the home planet. But why is it only extinct animals that turn up here?"

Kari came forward, her eyes on Ross rather than on the wolf. "Your arm . . ." she began.

Ross blinked, then recalled the wolf's jaws closing on his arm. And it did seem to be hurting a lot, now that he thought about it. He looked down to see the uniform sleeve in ribbons, black ribbons stained with red that dripped down the tatters. What he could see of the arm looked as shredded as the sleeve.

He considered it fairly calmly, priding himself on the fact that the sight of blood, even his own, had never bothered him much. This was going to be a problem, though. He didn't have any disinfectant, and obviously Kari wouldn't have any. Maybe Orl did; better ask him.

He turned toward Orl and then couldn't seem to stop turning. The world was spinning around him. He felt a strong arm around his waist and somehow Kari's face was there, and then the blackness of her face seemed to spread until it blocked out the sky.

He came awake slowly. There were distant voices, and after a few seconds he recognized them as Kari and Orl.

"It's a magic animal, then?" Kari said.

"It is certainly not a natural one," Orl said. "It has been manufactured; in your terms I assume that makes it magic."

"I wondered why there wasn't any blood in it."

"Nor does it have a digestive tract. It has no way of taking in food."

"Then why did it attack us?" Kari asked, puzzled. "If it didn't want us for food, there was no reason. And how does it live without food?"

"It doesn't live, any more than the Venntran cars do. It gets its power in the same way; I recognize these cells here as receptors."

"More magic," Kari said, disgusted.

Ross tried to sit up, and the world began spinning again. Kari and Orl hurried over, and Kari helped Ross prop his back against a tree. After a while the ground settled down and stopped whirling. His arm ached, but not much worse than his legs had done after their first day of walking. It was bandaged in strips of black cloth, obviously torn from the other sleeve, as the left arm was now bare.

"It isn't too bad a wound," Kari assured him. "It just bled a lot."

"We bandaged it as best we could," Orl said. "I have some drugs for use in such accidents, but since I didn't know how they might affect a different species, I was afraid to use them."

Ross thought about alien infections, but then realized that Orl and Kari had said the wolf was manufactured; it might not be as full of bacteria as a real one. And wasn't there some theory about alien microbes not being able to affect humans? It sounded reasonable.

Certainly, a corner of his mind informed him. *That's why the Indians were so resistant to smallpox.* Ross told it to go away and shut up.

He looked at the magic dire wolf, which had been carved apart, apparently by Orl's gun. The inside of the creature was a uniform gray, not unlike the color of the Gate buildings. There was neither blood nor bone.

"A robot?" Ross asked.

"As good a term as any," Orl agreed.

"As good as magic?"

"As good," Orl said, "but no better. This creature is equally magical to all of us; I do not understand how or why it was made. I have traced enough of its circuitry, however, to know that it is essentially a machine like the Venntran vehicles."

Then why a dire wolf? Ross thought. *"If someone, for some incomprehensible purpose, is making animals, why use an extinct animal from Earth? Commander Freff, this is more in your line; produce me an answer.*

The Commander didn't respond. Ross hadn't really expected him to, which he decided was a good thing. If the time came when he did start expecting answers from the Commander, he'd know that he really had problems. The thought of an insane computer came to mind, but how insane would a computer have to be to start creating Earth animals? And what would it use for a model?

"Quiet!" Kari's harsh whisper cut into Ross's thoughts. He saw that she was crouching low and motioning for Orl to do the same. Orl was looking around and fumbling in one of the pouches.

Then Ross heard it; the faint hissing that meant a

Venntran vehicle was hovering nearby. He tried to get his feet under him. Before he succeeded, a dozen black-uniformed barbarians crowded into the clearing. Nearly all of them held the triangle-barrelled guns in their hands.

"Do not move!" one of them ordered in a high, unpleasant voice. "We will not kill you unless you force us to."

Since Ross hadn't had much success in moving anyway, he sat back on the ground. At least these particular barbarians were talking instead of shooting on sight. If they were really going to kill, they must have had plenty of chances before they announced themselves.

"You will come with us," the same barbarian said. This was a blond young man, nearly as tall as Ross. This put him half a head above his companions. He motioned in the direction of the hissing noise. His exceptional size, Ross noticed, provided more space for dirt to lodge.

Ross had some trouble getting up, but he made it, and they were herded across the clearing, with their captors moving cautiously and very alertly. Surprisingly, they hadn't been disarmed; Ross's and Orl's guns were still in their pouches, and Kari still held her bow. At the moment, it didn't seem to make much difference.

Kari stumbled. As she recovered her balance, she shifted her grip to one end of the bow, using it as a cane to steady herself, as she limped behind Orl and Ross. Ross gave her a concerned look and was rewarded with a short firm headshake. Wondering what that meant, he walked on.

He found out what it meant as Kari spun around, the bow lashing out in a semicircle. One barbarian avoided the blow but sprawled backward on the ground as he

124

did so, a second was caught on the side of the head and knocked down, and Kari doubled over a third with a swift poke in the stomach. Before the rest of their captors realized what had happened, Kari was through the break in their line, stepping on one of the fallen men as she went, and disappearing into the trees.

A majority of the barbarians kept their guns trained on Orl and Ross, but two fired at Kari. She swerved and at first Ross thought she was hit, but then he saw that she had grabbed the briefcase with the remaining food and the dynamite, which their captors had left in the clearing. There were more shots, but now she was completely out of sight and the barbarians were firing at random. They stopped at a command from their leader, and there was no pursuit.

With no further incidents or words, Orl and Ross were marched to where not one but four Venntran vehicles hovered hissing above the grass near the road. No one touched them, but the guns never wavered, and Ross was certain that the slightest resistance would be fatal. He felt it was a bit shameful to not even attempt to escape after Kari had made hers good, but not shameful enough to get his head blown off trying.

Orl was ordered into one car, and Ross into another. Though Ross's car seemed no larger on the outside than the one the three of them had used before, four barbarians managed to fit themselves in while leaving considerable clearance between themselves and Ross. One drove while the others kept the weapons trained on Ross's middle. He noticed that the driver's movements were slow and uncertain when compared to Orl's.

They had traveled little more than a half hour when the remains of the vanished city appeared ahead of them. During the entire trip, not a word had been spoken. The four cars came to rest before the huge building Orl had indicated as the Temple. It reminded Ross of nothing more than a small version of the Vertical Assembly Building at Cape Kennedy. It was square, blocky, totally unornamented, totally business-like.

Ross was ordered out, and saw Orl emerging from a second car directly in front of him. As they had been in the forest, they were herded forward toward a spot in the wall of the building. Two barbarians stood about five feet apart in front of the wall, like Roman guards posted by a door, except there was no door.

Ross and Orl were prodded forward between the two guards, and as they were about to be walked into the wall, the door appeared, though not as abruptly as those on the Gate buildings. This time the motion was slow enough for Ross to see it. A four by seven foot section of wall directly between the two guards vanished in a motion that reminded Ross of a rectangular iris opening. There was motion on all sides of a central point, a sort of rectangular swirling, and as the swirling continued the central point opened out until the complete section was open. The dimensions of the corridor beyond were the same as those of the opening, so it looked more like a well-lighted rectangular tunnel than a hallway.

Ross and Orl were prodded into the corridor. Three of the barbarians followed close behind them, their guns still trained on their captives. Halfway down the corridor, the procession stopped and turned to face one wall. The swirling was repeated and they were pushed forward into a room, their captors following closely behind them.

The room was completely barren, as had been the corridor. The floor and ceiling and three of the walls were of the same featureless gray as the Gate buildings and the interior of the magic wolf. The fourth wall was black, as glossy as polished obsidian. It didn't appear to be transparent, and yet occasional dots of light appeared deep within it. Standing before it, Ross had the feeling that it could swallow him up, just as the Gate had done, except that this would be a mental rather than a physical swallowing. Strangely, he also had the feeling that he wanted to be swallowed up; absorbed, to abandon his problems and drift into oblivion.

"Present yourselves!" The voice was sharp, with a tenseness in it, as if the man was keeping control of himself only by an effort.

Ross was shoved roughly forward, dizziness assaulting him at the move, and he put out his left hand to break his fall. Stumbling, he went to his knees, and his hand, palm out, slapped against the night-black wall. Out of the corner of his eye, he saw Orl moving forward of his own accord, almost eagerly.

The instant Ross's hand touched the wall, a tingling sensation shot through his entire body. It felt somewhat like a mild electric shock except for its completeness. His entire body tingled, inside and out, and his mind felt the touch, like a distant itch, most of all.

He knelt there, awkwardly, off balance, for—how long? Seconds? Minutes? Hours? He couldn't tell; all outward senses deserted him as the tingling coursed through him. Then, though he was still facing the wall, he saw the three barbarians behind him. He saw them more clearly than he had seen them before, more sharply, as if his eyes were instruments of perfection, not missing a detail. And—he somehow saw them from all sides at once. They were turning. The gray wall swirled open again, and the black clad men strode through, and the wall resumed its gray blankness.

And then the vision was gone. The ebony wall was again before him.

From behind him there came the sound of shuffling feet. Cautiously, he twisted his head to look. The barbarians were turning. The wall was swirling open, the barbarians were striding through without a backward glance. The opening vanished as quickly as it appeared. For a moment, the tingling in Ross's body increased to an almost painful level, particularly in his right arm, and then, as suddenly as it had come, it was gone. Ross tumbled to the floor as if all the strength had gone out of him.

All right, Commander Freff, what now? he thought. *This must be the control center Orl was talking about, but I don't see his equipment around. Is this where we find out how insane a computer can be?*

He struggled to his feet, expecting the same waves of dizziness he had experienced before, but his mind was clear. He put a hand to his head, and abruptly realized that he had used his right arm. Experimentally, he moved the arm. It was sore, but he could use it.

Then words began to form in his mind. Not Venntran words, but English ones.

"At last!" the words said. "At last someone has come! Can you help me?"

CHAPTER 8

Ross looked around sharply. A super-computer that thought it could get much help out of him at present couldn't be too rational.

"You are the computer?" he asked in English. Orl, standing a yard away, looked over in surprise at the strange words.

More words appeared in Ross's mind. "The term will suffice," they said. "You do not seem to have a precise definition of a computer, and my structure can be fitted into your definition."

Orl's attention returned to the wall, and it was obvious that he was hearing something, too.

Again the thought formed, "Can you help me?" and this time, Ross realized, it was directed at Orl.

A series of rasping noises, similar to but not the same as the Venntran language they had been speaking, came from Orl. The language of Elsprag, evidently. Orl glanced toward Ross and said, "I told it that I was under the impression that it was we who needed the help, since these people are holding us prisoner."

This time, the computer evidently overcame whatever initial problems it had in communication with two dissimilar species, and Ross noted that the words seemed to be forming in his and Orl's minds simultaneously. "They are no problem. They were ordered to bring you here. They will do what they are told, as long as it is a task they are able to comprehend and provided their pleasures are not interfered with."

Between thoughts of what sort of insanity might be present in the computer, Ross wondered, as the words formed in his mind, why the computer talked so much the way he had always imagined computers would talk. And why English, when he knew Venntran? Then he realized that the computer was not actually talking at all. It was putting thoughts into his mind, and his mind was converting them to the form it expected. His mind was still trying to find something familiar in this alien world.

"You are not a Venntran," the words continued, and Ross knew they were aimed at Orl.

"My ancestors were Venntrans."

If computers could sigh, this one did. "You are from a colony world, then."

"Yes. From Elsprag."

There was a brief pause, and the tiny, elusive lights within the ebony wall seemed to take on a new activity.

"Elsprag," the voice said. "It was one of the last colonies. Two hundred eighty-three colonists at the time the Gates were sealed. Strange that one of the more populous worlds did not make first contact."

The words seemed to bring Orl back to life. "What happened?" he asked. "Why were the Gates closed? What happened to the Venntrans?"

As if the question was one the computer had been waiting for, there was a brief swirling in the blackness before them, and a picture formed on—in—the wall. As before, the image was incredibly clear and distinct, as if the image, like the words, was being imprinted directly on Ross's mind.

A saurian sat before a screen that looked like a small version of the wall in which the image was being formed. The Venntran, as far as Ross could tell, was

130

nearly identical to Orl. The almost nonexistent stump of vestigial tail was perhaps a bit more pronounced, and the crest was also slightly larger than Orl's, in addition to being either considerably darker than the rest of the body or being painted a darker shade of green.

Beyond the screen was a large bare room, perhaps a quarter the size of the ones in the Gate buildings. It was totally featureless except for a rectangular slab that was raised a few inches above the floor near the center of the room. Ross noticed that the air immediately surrounding the slab seemed to refract the light strangely. Behind the slab, the far walls of the room shifted deceptively.

On the screen an image was formed. It was a chaotic blur. Everything moved, and nothing was clear enough to identify, even if it had remained still. The colors were dark, mostly greys and deep reds, and their continuous swirling and shifting had a hypnotic quality.

From nowhere, a memory entered Ross's mind. There were no words; the computer was not speaking to him as it had before. There was simply a memory in his mind where there had been none before. He remembered what the Venntran was doing, and what the screen was. He was operating a Probe Gate, and the screen showed him where the other end of the probe existed. That is, the screen showed the operator where he would be if he fully activated the Gate and stepped through it. It did not tell him where he would be in reference to a stellar chart. For all the operator knew, it could be in the next solar system, or it could be circling a star in another galaxy.

Or, a new memory bubbled up to chill Ross's spine, it could be in another universe entirely. No one had ever proved that the places the Probe Gates reached were in the same physical universe as Venntra itself, though it was assumed. The only fact was that whatever places the Probe Gates reached, wherever or whenever they existed, instantaneous transmission to them was possible, as soon as the Gate was properly focussed and the transmission circuits engaged. When a suitable world was found, the Probe Gate was locked on to it, and Venntrans and equipment went through to build the permanent Gates. At the moment, only the vision circuits were operating, and the operator was having trouble even with those. Focussing was normally not that much trouble. A star popped into sight, a planet was located, the focus of the probe was shifted toward it, and minor adjustment were made. Trial and error was necessary to achieve the proper adjustment, but there was never a great variance.

This time was different.

The operator had been working for over an hour, and still the screen showed nothing but swirling chaos. Even from space the world had not been completely in focus. What had looked like greyish clouds had covered everything, and the boundary between the planet and the blackness of space around it had not been distinct. There had been something odd about that sun, too. But as the focus had shifted in toward the planet, the blurring had increased.

The operator wondered in some exasperation where his Gate had emerged this time. Had it reached out beyond its effective range? One school of thought held that this was to be expected eventually; if it had finally happened, he'd have all the Gate scientists on Venntra poking around his machine. Or had the probe, as others speculated, penetrated into another universe, with different physical laws than those of Venntra?

Though the Venntran himself was only a trifle irritated by his problem, Ross felt a chill once again, and a probably inaccurate line from *Alice In Wonderland* floated to the surface of his mind; something about believing one impossible thing before breakfast. He wondered how many more impossible things he was going to be called on to believe here.

Again the Venntran's seven-fingered hands moved across the blank area below the screen, and the image became even less coherent. Ross, as the Venntran's hands moved, felt his own hands moving, as if he was being absorbed by the mind of the Venntran.

Abruptly, his mind was split in two. One part remained outside, in the room with Orl, while the other part was pulled into the Venntran's mind. He could feel the seven-fingered hands, the weight of the outsize head, a dozen other sensations for which Ross Allan had no names. Now he could see the markings on the panel beneath the screen. To Venntran eyes, they were clear and distinct. A dozen markings, all representing separate controls for the Probe Gate, controls that appeared as tiny, glowing lines that shifted as the Venntran's fingers passed across them.

Another thought came, and for a moment Ross couldn't tell whether it had come to himself or to the Venntran. *Perhaps,* the thought said, *what I am seeing is the true image.*

The Venntran's hands moved swiftly across the panel again, and the patterns of glowing lines altered radically. As they did, the jumble of whirling images on the screen before him altered just as radically. For just an instant, everything sharpened and came into focus. The swirling and shifting didn't stop, nor the images transmute into something recognizable. Instead of blurred chaos, there was, for a moment, sharply defined chaos. It still made no sense, but now he could see precisely what it was that made no sense.

In the same instant, the air above the slab in the center of the room darkened and filled with the same swirling shapes that filled the screen. A pulsing came from the slight discontinuity around the slab that was a shield, a precaution used on all Probe Gates. The wall beyond the slab blurred and shimmered, and the darkness that hovered over the slab seemed to expand and rush out into the room.

It was impossible, of course. The shield was impenetrable to all known forms of matter and energy.

All *known* forms. . . .

Instantly, the Venntran's hands darted across the controls. The image in the screen faded into blackness, and the darkness hovering over the slab faded into nothingness. The shield once again glimmered almost invisibly.

The Venntran looked around the featureless room. It was empty, as it was supposed to be. He checked the screen again. It had returned to the bottomless blackness that indicated it was not working.

Yet the Venntran felt uneasy. To Ross, still inhabiting both his own and the Venntran's minds, it was a familiar feeling, the kind he often had when sitting alone in his apartment late at night, his mind conjuring up invisible and lurking horrors for a story. There was the feeling that if he looked around quickly enough, one of the horrors would be standing behind him, just fading from view. The feeling that no matter what his rational mind told him, there was something else in the room with him.

It was the same thing, he realized, that he had felt in

the car with Orl and Kari. The feeling that *something* was out there, waiting.

To the Venntran, the feeling was unprecedented and totally senseless. Since it was irrational and therefore unimaginable, it was doubly terrifying. In all his life, there had been nothing to prepare him for it. Even the terror itself, rising suddenly out of nowhere, was a source of additional terror. In a logical, organized work there were dangers, of course, but they were logical and well-defined and could be avoided or at least minimized by proper action. Such dangers didn't leap at you out of nowhere. There were *reasons* for them!

But there was no reason for this one. Nothing was in the room. Nothing could have come through Probe Gate, even in the few seconds it had been locked on the planet. Nothing could travel through a scanner beam, and the transmission beams had not been activated; they were never activated until a new world had been thoroughly scanned for possible dangers. If something had traveled through the scanner beam, it couldn't penetrate the shield, and would have been snatched back to its source when the Probe Gate field was shut off. And the monitors had registered nothing.

There was no possible reason for the terror, but it was still there.

The Venntran began to make sounds. Had he been a human, the sounds would have been short, sharp intakes of breath, moans and bleats of terror as every sound, every sight and touch meant a new source of terror.

This, Ross realized, must be very much like what Orl had experienced when he had run screaming from their vehicle. No wonder he'd run. It was similar to the terror that Ross himself had experienced, but more intense. More intense, at least, to the Venntran. To Ross, his

135

mind still split between the Venntran and himself, there was a curious detachment. He was experiencing what the Venntran was experiencing, but at the same time he was standing in a room over ten thousand years removed from the Venntran, watching the saurian cower and tremble.

Then it was over. The images in the screen wavered and blurred as if they were going out of focus. The ebon wall was again before him. Ross Allen's mind was again all his, no longer shared by the long-dead Venntran. The memories, though, were still there. They were only memories—and not even his own—yet his entire body went limp for an instant as they poured over him. The instant passed. The memories remained, but became distant. No matter how terrifying they might seem they were only, really, a very vivid motion picture. Ross pushed himself away from the wall and for the first time since the images had appeared, he looked around the room.

Orl lay stretched on the floor. His eyes were open, with a glassy look in them. He was breathing heavily and lying perfectly still, as he had in the aftermath of the terror he had experienced in the car.

Ross went over and knelt at his side, but he knew there was nothing he could do about the saurian's condition.

"Do not concern yourself," the words spoke in Ross's mind. The computer was talking to him again.

"He will return to consciousness soon," the words continued. "I am monitoring his vital functions. I terminated the sequence for him when it became clear that further data would have produced serious damage to his mind."

Ross turned to face the ebon wall. "Did you do this to us before? Out there somewhere?"

Was this the computer's insanity? Did it somehow take pleasure in driving its creators insane with fear?

"I did not," the words in Ross's mind said, "but I did."

"What . . ." Ross began, but stopped as the words repeated themselves.

"I did not, but I did."

No, the words did not precisely match the thoughts. The two "I's" in the thought were not the same. Both referred to what Ross thought of as the computer, but there was a difference. One seemed somehow more personal, more closely tied to the computer-entity. The second was still associated with the computer, but there was an impersonal touch.

Then the difference clarified. It was as if a human had said, "I did not do it; my hand did it."

There was a feeling of agreement from the computer.

"I don't understand," Ross said.

"Nor do I," the computer said into his mind. "I know only that what you just saw was the beginning."

But the beginning of what? Of computerized schizophrenia? Was the vague, undefined "thing" the equivalent of the mysterious voices that schizophrenics heard, giving them messages that only they could hear? But why? Why would such a creation lose control over part of itself?

Another vision began to form in the wall, but Ross pulled back, suspicious. "Orl can't take any more of this."

"Orl is unconscious," the words said. "I speak only to you."

Again, a thousand tiny lights glittered deep within

the wall, then faded. Ross felt it reaching out to touch his mind, and could not avoid the touch.

The blackness before him faded and became an image. A Venntran sat alone in a room. As before, the room was barren, the walls dead and gray. It was, according to his memory, another room in this building, an observation room from which any spot on the planet could be seen. There was a chair and another of the blackened screens, but this was not the screen to a Probe Gate. Probe Gates no longer existed. They had been destroyed.

The Venntran was frightened. She was, Ross realized, a female. She had been terrified for many days. She had not slept, for she was afraid to sleep. While she remained awake, she could fight off the terror, but when she slept, it swept over her like an irresistible tide. What turned the fear into unreasoning terror was the simple fact that there was no object for it. It was nameless, indefinable, everpresent. Her eyes told her that she was alone in the room, but her fear said that there was something else, alien and malevolent, in the room with her.

There was no escape. All Gates leaving Venntra had been sealed by the computer in order to contain whatever it was that had swept over the planet like a windborne plague. The first death from fright and shock, had been the operator of the Probe Gate. From him, it had spread.

Future shock, Ross decided, or something quite similar. The Venntrans' every waking moment was a nightmare, and not one of them had ever had a nightmare before. Not one had any idea that nightmares existed, and now they were living in one.

They didn't live long. Their rigid, logical minds, so

138

successful in tracking down and making use of every law of science, could not withstand the totally illogical thing which appeared in their midst. Their minds snapped, and their bodies followed.

Once again Ross found himself split in two. A portion of his mind was with the Venntran while a second portion remained in his own body, observing, remembering, thinking.

He felt the terror as the Venntran felt it, and screamed in pain. To the Venntran, despite her iron control, the fear was a physical pain, and Ross saw that it would not last much longer. Despite the agony, the Venntran continued to operate the screen before her, shifting from scene to scene. But all the scenes were the same. Everywhere, there was death. A few Venntrans, mostly females, were still alive, but it was only a matter of time.

After a time, the Venntran turned off the screen. She had known from the first that it was no use. There was nowhere on Venntra to flee, and there was no way to escape the planet with the Gates closed. Not that fleeing the planet would do any good; where she could flee, the terror could follow.

Abruptly, as if a twig had been snapped, the mind of the Venntran was gone, and Ross was alone in his mind. He stood again in the gray-walled room before a black, star-flecked screen. His mind and body ached from the memory of the experience he had gone through, and he knew that in those few minutes he had seen the end of a civilization.

"But what was it?" he asked when he had recovered enough to speak.

"I do not know," the computer said. "You have been given the only information I possess."

"But it was something that came through the Probe Gate? That was the cause?"

"It appears that it was."

"But how did it cause the fear?"

"That is its nature."

"But how?" Ross repeated. "What was it doing?"

"That is its nature," the computer said.

Then Ross understood, The computer was saying "It is magic". The being, alien, *thing* was as far removed from what the computer was equipped to understand as the computer was beyond Ross's ability to understand. The being had come from an alien universe where the laws of our universe did not apply. By its very existence, it created terror in the minds of beings in our universe with which it came in contact.

Was it a living being? Did its contacts with beings like Ross and Orl cause it the same terror that it caused in them? Or did terror have a meaning to it? Was it even a living being? Could it simply be a dislodged piece of that alien universe?

Suddenly, despite the lingering ache in Ross's body and mind, he grinned. *A corollary to Clarke's Third Law,* he thought. *Natural phenomena, sufficiently alien, are indistinguishable from either advanced science or magic.*

"When the last of the Venntrans died," he asked the computer, "what happened?"

"The alien became a part of me."

"It still exists, then? The same creature?"

"It exists as a part of me."

"Does it have control over you?"

"It is a part of me."

"Can it be destroyed?" *And why,* Ross thought, *am I standing here playing Twenty Questions with a com-*

140

puter? There must be a more profitable way to spend my time. But he couldn't think of one.

"That part of me can be destroyed," the computer said.

"But will whatever came through from that other universe be destroyed as well?"

"I cannot say with exactitude."

"Okay, then; what are the odds of it being destroyed?"

"I have no way of determining them."

"If that part of you is destroyed, will you yourself survive? Will you still be capable of unsealing the Gates?"

"Yes. But I will unseal no Gates until it is proven that the creature has been destroyed. I will not take a chance on letting it reach other worlds. That was the reason for sealing the Gates in the beginning."

"You wish that part of you destroyed, then."

"Yes. As long as it is a part of me, I will be irrational."

"And that's the help you asked for."

"Yes."

Ross sighed. He was positive the computer could have told him all this without all the questioning, but apparently it wanted to be perverse.

"How do we handle the destruction?" he asked.

"You must travel to that part of me and remove the safety devices. Destruction will follow automatically."

"Why can't you remove the device yourself? You seem able to do about everything else."

"My directives forbid it," came the words in Ross's mind. Or had that word been "conscience" instead of "directives"?

"What about the barbarians? Why haven't you had them do it?"

"I have tried. They seem incapable of understanding the action required."

A noise made Ross turn around. Orl was moving slowly, his eyes blinking, the glazed look gone. Ross moved to his side and helped him to stand up. Orl's face was as unreadable as ever, but his motions reminded Ross of a man with a severe hangover.

Orl looked around uncertainly. "The Probe Gate," he began unsteadily. "There was something. . . . I must inform. . . ."

"He is still in the mind of the Probe Gate operator," the words came in Ross's mind. "He will return to normal in a short time."

"Isn't there anything you can do for him?"

"He is in no danger. I am monitoring his vital functions."

"You said that before." Ross remembered his injured arm; that had been a vital function. He moved the arm, slowly at first. There was no pain and he stretched it farther, flexing the muscle. There was still no pain, only a slight tingle.

"You may unwrap it," the computer told him.

"What did you do to it?"

"I repaired it."

"But how. . . ." Ross began.

"It is one of my functions. You were analyzed and the proper stimulation applied."

Ross thought of the night they had spent in the Gate building, remembering how Orl had told he and Kari to place their hands against a spot on the wall so their metabolism could be analyzed and food provided.

"Rossallen?" It was Orl's voice, sounding normal again. "What happened?"

"I'm not sure," Ross said, "but I gather you listened a little to closely to what our friend was saying." He gestured at the screen.

Orl blinked and shook his head as if to clear it of lingering images. "I believe you are right. But what was it? Is that what destroyed Venntra?"

"Apparently it was. But not even the computer knows what it was. Or what it is, I should say."

"It still exists, then." Orl didn't sound very surprised.

"Somehow, once all the Venntrans were dead, it merged with the computer."

Orl jerked away from the screen.

"It is not in this room," the words said into their minds. "It exists in a different part of me."

"Whatever and wherever it is, it's responsible for what happened to us," Ross said. He went on to explain what he had learned, ending by saying "And after we've destroyed the Wicked Witch of the West, the Great Oz here will grant our wishes and send us home."

Orl looked puzzled, but Ross seemed to hear a ghostly chuckle in his mind.

"But what about the other things?" Orl asked. "The barrier? The animals? The disappearing buildings?"

"I/it is responsible," came the words. "The barrier was mine. I did not wish you to wander so far that you could not be found."

"But you might have killed us!" Ross protested.

"The barrier would not have killed you," the computer said. "The buildings you refer to were energy constructs. At the time of Venntra's destruction, very few buildings were physically constructed. I contained the patterns for all food, clothing, and shelter. Except for the Gate buildings and a few others retained from earlier times, all structures were energy constructs. To maintain them requires large amounts of energy. I did not maintain them after the Venntrans were destroyed, but when the barbarians arrived, I produced the buildings for them. Since you two have arrived, however, that other part of me has been taking more and more of my available energy. I was not able to maintain the buildings."

"The animals!" Ross said. "Is that what your other half has been using the energy for? To create those phony animals?"

"Partially. I do not know what it is all being used for."

"But why the animals? And what's it using for a pattern?"

"I do not know why," the voice said, and Ross thought he could detect a plaintive note to it. "It is using the images from your own mind for patterns."

"Is it trying to kill us before we can help you?" Ross asked.

"It is acting according to its nature," the computer replied, and Ross realized that there wasn't much point in continuing that line of questions.

"Maybe it just likes me," he said a trifle bitterly. "It's just reflecting back what it finds in my mind; what it thinks I want to see. But why doesn't it create animals from your mind?" he asked Orl. "Why pick on me?"

"I would have no reason to think of animals," Orl suggested.

"Neither do I. I just—dream—about them." As he spoke the words, everything fell into place. There was no Venntran word for dreams or imagination. Venntrans, Elspragans, Leeanese, every one but Ross, simply didn't dream. His was the only mind inhabited by a menagerie of animals from which the being could take its patterns. He wondered if there was any way to control his thoughts.

"You said this creature could be destroyed," he said. If he was going on some sort of dangerous mission for an alien computer, he at least wanted some assurance of success.

He didn't get one. "It is possible," the computer said, "but I can not guarantee the destruction." There was a pause, and the distant lights in the blackened screen before them seemed to take on renewed activity.

"It is becoming imperative that you try, soon," the voice said. "That part of me has begun drawing additional energy. If it continues increasing at the present rate, it will shortly destroy the planet."

CHAPTER 9

Ross stared at the flickering blackness. Some of the terror of the millenia-dead Venntrans seeped into his mind, cold and gray. He knew he had not misheard, but he asked anyway.

"Did we hear you correctly? This thing in you is going to destroy Venntra?"

"If it continues to draw energy as it is now beginning to do."

"But the safeguards . . . you said that before even that one section of you could be destroyed, we had to remove safety devices."

"That is true. The safeguards ensure that no section of me can be overloaded, because supplementary power can be drawn from other sections. To destroy one section, it must be isolated from the general power flow; the alien use of power will then overload the power supply for that section. But I/it now threatens to overload the entire system."

"But won't that just cause the power supply to fail?" Ross asked. "Aren't there other safeguards to prevent an explosion?"

"Of course, but you must remember that much time has passed. If the power center was functioning normally, there would be no problem. In the years since the Venntrans were destroyed, however, there has been a gradual lessening of efficiency of the entire system. Not all component failures and resulting damage has been repairable by me. With the power center in its present condition, my calculations show that the fields which contain the energy-producing reactions will break down before the safety devices act to shut down the reaction. The result will be a surge of uncontrolled power on a vast scale. Your mind contains knowledge of nuclear bombs; I would judge that all the nuclear energy available in your world is less than that generated by this Venntran power system."

Blowups happen, Ross thought to himself, *even here.* "But surely you control some master override that can be used to shut off the energy before it explodes."

"My directives oppose self-destruction. If the power supply was shut down, I would cease to exist. Breakdown of the containing fields will also cause me to cease to exist, but at a later time. I would, in your terms, have longer to live by allowing the explosion to occur."

"But you'd be saving countless lives!"

"My directives call for the preservation of intelligent Venntran life before my own—but you and the other barbarians are not Venntrans."

"What about Orl, then? He is part of the Venntran species."

"My directives do not include lives of colonists; it was not considered necessary."

"With the power supply shut off," Orl broke in, "the computer and all its aspects would be inoperative. There would be no power to the Gates. We would be isolated on Venntra forever—with the creature of fear existing among us."

"Forever or until someone comes to Venntra with a starship," Ross corrected. "Which could be next year or not for a million years, and I suppose the creature could still be in existence here."

"That is true," the words in their minds said. "There

is no reason to believe that I/it will ever cease to exist."

"Unless we remove the safety devices so it will blow up," Ross said.

"Even then," the computer warned, "there is no guarantee of its destruction."

"But it's our only chance, I guess," Ross said glumly. "How long do we have?"

"It is impossible to predict accurately. If the present trend continues, breakdown will occur in approximately one day."

Ross's stomach lurched. "In that case," he said, "I suppose we'd better be going. What do we have to do?"

"You must reach that section of me to be destroyed, and you must deactivate the safeguards."

"I know that. How do we locate the section? How do we get to it? How do we recognize a safeguard, so we don't deactivate the company water cooler instead?"

"I will guide you." Something appeared on the surface of the star-flecked blackness before them. Two somethings, in fact. They appeared to be discs about an inch and a half in diameter, their color the same indeterminate gray that seemed to make up everything connected to the computer except the vision screens. In the center of each was a raised figure of some kind.

"Take these," the words spoke into their minds.

Ross blinked. The discs appeared to be images, and anyway how could a solid object exist inside the solid screen? He reached forward, expecting to touch the surface of the screen as he had done before. Instead, his hand melted into the surface as if it were a dense shadow, and closed over a quite solid object, a medallion of some kind. His hand tingled as he touched it.

He withdrew his hand, grasping the medallion. There was a slight resistance, as if he was pulling it from a weak magnetic field. He handed it to Orl, who had been standing silently through most of the exchange, and reached into the screen again for the second disc. Removing it, he examined it with interest. The raised figure was a representation of the building they were now in; the Temple, as Orl called it. But it was more than a simple bas-relief form. Somehow, a three-dimensional image of the building had been incorporated into a flat disc. As if to demonstrate its true nature, the image vanished for a moment, to be replaced by a tiny area of sparking blackness.

Then, almost before it had gone, the image of the building returned.

Ross and Orl placed the medallions around their necks. The chains, of the same gray material as everything else, seemed to squirm and adjust themselves, and then were still.

The wall opposite the ebon screen swirled open, and the three who had escorted them into the room stood waiting, with an oddly expectant look. For the first time, Ross noticed the thin gray strand around each neck.

"Yes," the words formed silently in his mind, "all who enter here have similar devices. I have made yours larger, to indicate your status."

Then more words formed, to be heard by the three who awaited he and Orl in the corridor. "Wherever these two go, whatever they do, they are my messengers. They speak for me in all things. You will do what they request."

The three looked at Ross and Orl, their eyes fastening on the medallions. They said nothing, but a surge of anger rushed across each face.

"You will escort them to the House Which Is Not

149

Entered," the voice went on as they stepped into the corridor.

There was brief hesitation, but no open rebellion. The faces, however, were expressive. Ross wondered uneasily how long the computer would be able to hold these barbarians' loyalty now that its energy crisis had deprived them of most of their city and probably of other benefits. He and Orl followed the three down the corridor and they emerged into the sunlight. The sun was nearly overhead, which meant they had been in the Temple—five hours? Was it possible? A check of his watch convinced Ross that it was possible, though it had seemed as though no more than an hour had passed. The visions, that reliving of fragments of Venntran lives, must have taken longer than he had thought.

As they walked, Ross had to stifle an impulse to laugh. Here he was, Ross Allen, Interstellar Agent, with his faithful companion the talking dinosaur, despatched by an alien computer on a mission to save a planet. It wasn't a well-populated planet, but it was a planet nevertheless, an entire world, and it was populated by himself at the very least. He was going out to locate a relic of a civilization that had died while men on Earth were building their first cities, and it all suddenly seemed unbelievable. An improbable mission, to say the least, and if they failed, the Universe would disavow all knowledge of their existence.

Where, he wondered, was Commander Freff? This was the sort of thing the Commander excelled in; it really shouldn't be entrusted to a fallible mortal like Ross Allen. Just how sure was he that this was all real, anyway? Maybe back there in the dim past when he had driven the bulldozer across that slab, something actually had blown up, and all of these last few days were only his hospital nightmares.

He supposed it didn't matter. It felt real, and he had better act as if it was. Nightmares didn't need his attention; reality did. He forced his attention into the proper channel. They were out in the open, walking past one of the hissing cars, near which stood a half dozen of the black-clad barbarians. Ross thought he recognized most of them from their capture this morning, and they didn't look at all friendly when they recognized him. He hoped the medallions were as potent as the computer seemed to believe.

One of the three escorts started to say something to the leader of the group by the car, but whether it was "Get out of the way!" or "Sic 'em!" Ross never knew. Something thumped into the ground a dozen feet ahead of them, only a few feet from the car. There was a hissing, spitting sound, and Ross recognized it with horror.

"Everybody down!" he shouted, spinning around and knocking Orl backward to the ground. He stared at the arrow with the stick of dynamite laced tightly to it. For a moment his impulse was to rush up and throw it as far as he could, but the sputtering fuse was almost gone and he'd never reach it.

Yelling "Down!" again, he dived for the ground himself, pressing his body tightly against the soil and trying to burrow his head into it. He was bringing up his arms over his head when the explosion came.

It was deafening. The ground shook and his ears hurt.

From somewhere came a distant voice: "This way!"

Ross looked up. Their escort of three was on the ground several yards away. They were picking themselves up shakily. The cluster of six near the vehicle was also on the ground. Two of them were making scrabbling motions in the dirt, but the others lay still, and looked as though they wouldn't be getting up for some time, if ever. They hadn't been on top of the explosion, but they had been far too close to it.

Again the voice came: "Hurry up! This way!"

Ross recognized it, helped by the fact that there was only one person it could be.

Kari.

Ross scrambled to his feet, looking around frantically. Orl apparently recognized the voice, too, for he was also looking in all directions as he struggled to his feet. Finally Ross spotted her. Somehow she had climbed to the top of one of the other buildings about a hundred yards away and now stood near one corner, bow in hand, waving to them.

"No!" Ross shouted, waving his hands at her. "They're letting us. . . ."

"Watch out behind you!" Kari shouted, snatching up another arrow from the roof next to her. Even at this distance, Ross could see that it was far too fat for a normal arrow. Then he saw a small flame in her hand, and a moment later the arrow was being pulled back.

"Don't do it!" Ross shouted.

Then he heard the sounds behind him and turned to look. Another half dozen of the barbarians had appeared from somewhere and were bearing down on him. They looked fearful as well as angry, but they were coming, bringing out their guns as they came.

At the same time, he heard the swish and thump of the arrow as it shot over his head and stuck in the ground about halfway between him and the advancing barbarians. His impulse to run over and throw it away was considerably shorter this time, and he and Orl again dived to the ground.

Again, after no more than a couple of seconds' sputtering, there was an explosion, even more deafening than the first. Kari obviously had solved the problem of timing the fuse.

Ross scrambled up again, his ears ringing. This time the barbarians had dived to the ground, apparently, for none seemed to be permanently injured. They all seemed groggy and stunned, however, as they stumbled to their feet and looked dazedly at the hole the dynamite had made.

"Come on!" Ross said, grabbing one of Orl's arms and hoisting him the rest of the way to his feet. "I don't think those medallions are going to save us now."

Half dragging Orl, Ross started toward the vehicle, but after covering only a few feet, he veered to the left, toward the building where Kari stood. The vehicle was no longer hovering and hissing. It was still hissing, but it was tilted sideways, one side touching the ground.

As they ran, Orl picking up speed and steadiness as they went, Ross shot a swift look to the rear. No one was after them, at least at that precise second. The barbarians had struggled to their feet. They were still dazed, but would probably be clear-headed enough to use their guns before long. Then he and Orl were behind the building Kari had fired from, and Ross had no idea of what to do next. It was a half-mile across open ground to the nearest point of forest, and he knew he could never make it in time, even by himself. Trying to get Orl across alive was out of the question.

A moment later, Kari dropped lithely to the ground a few yards away, and Ross noticed a series of handholds leading upward to the roof near where she had come down. He could see that four of the arrows in her quiver had sticks of dynamite attached, and she held the lighter in the same hand she held the bow.

"Let's go!" she said, waving toward the distant forest. "I still have four of your magic sticks. That should hold them back long enough to. . . ."

"They were letting us go!" Ross said, bitterly. "Until you came along, we didn't need to hold them back."

Abruptly a memory appeared in Ross's mind, and he stopped speaking. There was no voice, just a memory. It had appeared just as the others had appeared out of nowhere while he had joined minds with long-ago Venntrans in the computer room. He recalled now that about fifty yards to the right of where they stood was another building, which contained the entrance to the remains of an ancient underground transit system. The system had been built and used long before energy constructs had replaced physical structures, and the barbarians, Ross somehow knew, were not aware of what the building contained.

The computer, he decided, must be feeding him information through the medallion; there was no other way he could know all this. He looked around and spotted the building. It was gray like all the others, but it was smaller and instead of being square and blocky, it was cylindrical and blocky. Orl, he noticed, was looking in the same direction.

"This way!" Ross ordered, and sprinted toward the building. "Hurry up!" he shouted back at Orl and Kari as he saw that the barbarians were no longer staring at the hole in the ground but going after their pistols, most of which seemed to have been blown out of their hands by the explosion. From another building beyond the Temple, more barbarians were emerging.

Orl started after Ross, and after starting off in the

154

direction of the forest, Kari followed, looking puzzled. As Ross neared the building, a rectangular area of the wall began the familiar swirling motion and a moment later there was an opening. This one, Ross noticed, was not as clearly or sharply defined as the ones in the Temple had been. The edges were blurred, and there was an unevenness about them. Age, he wondered, or damage? And what difference did it make?

He skidded to a stop inside the opening and looked back. The barbarians had their guns and were moving forward at a nervous jog. The guns were pointed generally at Ross and the others, but nobody fired. The computer trying to hold them back? Even if that were so, it wouldn't succeed for long. Kari and Orl piled through the opening as the first of the pursuers overcame whatever restraint he had felt, and fired. There was the familiar crackling sound, and an elliptical gouge appeared in the dirt a few feet from the opening. The man must still be a little groggy, Ross thought, and a good thing, too.

With all three of them safely inside, the opening swirled shut.

As the entrance vanished, so did the light, and they were in total darkness. The only sound other than their own breathing was a faint crackling coming from the wall. The barbarians apparently were still firing at the vanished entrance, and Ross wondered if it would hold up long enough for he and Kari and Orl to feel their way out of this mausoleum.

As he wondered, an answer appeared in his mind in the form of a vague reassurance that, from this quarter at least, there was no reason for immediate concern.

At the same time, another memory appeared, and Ross knew that their destination, that section of the computer which they must destroy, was perhaps half a Venntran day's travel from where they now were. The transit tunnels provided the easiest access, and he wondered if this building might be the House Which Is Not Entered, where the computer had been sending them. A vague flicker in the back of his mind seemed to say that it was.

A dozen questions came to Ross's mind, but any answering memories were blotted out by Kari's voice.

"Where are we? Why did you bring us in here? How do we get out?" The voice sounded nervous, and echoed hollowly in the darkness.

"We don't get out," Ross said, still angry at Kari's interference in the computer's plans. "We go ahead."

"How? Does your magic let you see in the dark?"

"I don't know, but we can't go outside. We'd be killed in a second, thanks to you."

"What are you talking about?" She sounded both annoyed and a little apprehensive. "If it hadn't been for me . . ."

"If it hadn't been for you," Ross said nastily, "we'd have had plenty of time to find out about this place before we went inside, and had the good wishes of the locals as well!" Even as he spoke, however, he wondered a bit about that last.

"But . . ."

"They were letting us go! Do you understand that?"

"No, I don't! They've been trying to kill us ever since we got here, and. . . ."

"Well, dammit, they quit trying, until you provoked them again! Orl and I had things all settled, until you butted in and ruined things!"

Then Orl's rasping voice came from a few feet away. "Don't worry, Kari," he said. "Your intentions were of

156

the best; it was just that there were things you didn't know."

Ross felt a twinge of guilt. After all, he wasn't positive that the barbarians would have obeyed the computer; he'd been worrying about the possibility that they wouldn't when Kari opened fire. A vision of Kari straining to pull him out of the barrier field rose before his eyes. If she had waited then before acting, he and Orl could both be dead. The computer had said the field wasn't fatal, but Ross wasn't entirely convinced.

"Sorry," he said into the darkness. "It wasn't your fault. You couldn't know."

"Well, if you didn't want to be rescued, I'm sorry I did it." Kari's voice was sullen, but considerably more subdued than Ross had ever heard it before. "And what couldn't I have known?"

"That I was right when I told Orl he should have stayed captured," Ross said, and chuckled. "The ruler of Venntra is indeed a computer of sorts, and it sent us on a mission." He related to Kari their adventures in the computer room.

"Then those funny discs you're wearing are more magic," she said. "Are they as good as Orl's magic equipment?"

"Better, hopefully," Ross said. "Incidentally, how did you get to the city? Even you couldn't have walked the distance in the time we were in the computer room."

Some of Kari's old assurance was in her voice as she replied, and Ross could visualize her grinning at him in the darkness. "I ran across a Venntran with one of those funny riding animals," she said. "After I killed him, another bunch chased me in a car, but your magic sticks took care of that. Frightened the animal into going faster than usual, too. I turned it loose in the forest and walked into the city. Nobody paid any attention to me when I came in; they all seemed interested in the Temple. I didn't know where you were, but Orl thought he'd be taken to the Temple, so I climbed up on that roof and watched until you came out." She continued, sounding subdued again. "I'm sorry I spoiled things for you."

"It came out all right," Ross said. "The computer was sending us here anyway, but I assumed we'd have some light when we got here." He wondered how they were going to be able to see to get anywhere. Several years ago, he had taken a tour of Mammoth Cave, and the guides had given a demonstration of total darkness by turning out all the lights while they were underground. It was like that here, and Ross felt the same helplessness.

But even as he stood there, wondering if he dared move, he realized that the darkness was no longer total. A dim light, almost like the glow of a firefly, suffused the air. There was no source as far as he could tell; the light came out of the air itself. Then he noticed Orl's medallion, and his own. The image of the Temple was no longer displayed. Instead, the star-flecked blackness of the vision screen filled their centers. The medallions were not glowing, but the light seemed strongest near them. It gradually brightened until they could see large objects as far away as a hundred feet, but at its brightest Ross would have cheerfully traded it for a good flashlight or lantern.

More magic. He couldn't help but wonder if he would ever have a chance to use any of these gimmicks in a Commander Freff adventure. The Commander's fans would undoubtedly love them—always assuming that the series would sell and provide the Commander with some fans.

They were in a single large room. Across the room from them, opposite the spot they had entered, was a stairway leading down into more blackness. Together, Ross and Orl started across the intervening floor toward the stairs. Kari followed, looking considerably less assertive than usual. As they walked, more memories darted across Ross's mind, and he sensed that Orl was receiving them as well. Or could you receive memories? Anyway, memories were appearing to both of them. The underground system dated back to a time before energy constructs were possible, before the Gates were discovered, while Venntra was still sending out starships though conventional space. It had been built even before the computer.

No, that was not quite true. The very beginnings of the computer had existed at the time; its first primitive sections had been used to control the transit system. Over the centuries and millenia, as the computer increased in size and power, as energy constructs were used more and more for every phase of life, as the computer was used to construct food and clothing in Venntran homes instead of operating factories, the need for a transit system had dwindled. Eventually it was abandoned. Some of the space in the abandoned system was used in the construction of additional computer sections. The memories were unclear about the reasons for this; it seemed to have something to do with the fact that the computer banks could not be energy constructs and therefore should not be built on the surface. Perhaps Orl would find a logical sequence there, but Ross merely accepted it as incomprehensible fact.

The importan part of the memories was the one that told Ross that one of the last computer sections to be built before the final, "ultimate", control center had been installed was the one which was now possessed by the thing that had come through the Probe Gate. It also told him the location of the section.

They descended the steps, the dim glow traveling with them. When they were halfway down, a wide, flat-bottomed tunnel came into view at the foot of the stairs. It vanished into darkness in both directions. As they reached the bottom, Ross glanced back up the way they had come. There, too, there was only darkness.

A picture from an old comic book flashed into Ross's mind, and he smiled at it. "If we find old Shazam down here," he muttered in English, I'll *know* this is all a nightmare."

Orl and Kari looked at him strangely but said nothing.

They turned to the left and began walking. The tunnel was a good hundred feet wide and nearly as high. The light that followed them only occasionally showed them the roof over their heads, and unless they walked in the middle only one wall could be seen. In most places, the rock and dirt through which the tunnel had been carved were still visible behind the thin, nearly transparent substance that lined the walls. The liner had cracked in a few spots, allowing dirt to spill into the tunnel. Near the cracks, the liner changed from near transparency to a milky white. At one point, Ross picked up a piece of the liner that had broken away entirely. Around the edges it was opaque and white, while the center was still clear. It was no thicker than a piece of tin, though far heavier, and Ross experimentally tried to bend it. The white part crumbled into dust, but the transparent portion that remained was a rigid as steel. Another gadget for Commander Freff? No, nothing as practical as a formula for a superior plastic would interest the Commander. He was a romantic secret agent, not an industrial spy. Ross sailed the piece against the wall fifty feet away, where it struck with a thud and dropped to the floor.

Twice in the hours that followed, they had to climb over huge piles of rock and dirt that partially blocked the tunnel. In both cases, Kari helped Ross in the climb, and they both helped Orl, who seemed even less well designed for climbing than he was for sneaking quietly through trees. The tunnel branched, but their memories kept them on the right path.

They had been on the move for hours, and Ross was ready for another rest stop, when they came to a wall extending fully across the tunnel. As they approached, they expected some part of it to begin swirling and an opening to appear, but nothing happened.

"What's wrong?" Kari asked.

"It's not that type of wall," Ross answered, dredging his knowledge from his computer-implanted memories. "This was left over from the original transit system, as a guard against the energy powering the system." *Like a fire door*, he thought, *or a ship's bulkhead*, and realized that neither simile was going to mean anything to Kari. "It was built before those swirling doors were invented."

"Then how do we get past it?" Kari asked. "Can we use your pistols to cut through it?"

An answering memory surfaced in Ross's mind. The energy the pistols produced was closely related to the energy which had powered the transit system, and the doors had been specifically designed to withstand that form of energy. "Not unless that door has weakened a lot over the years," he said. "And it doesn't look much like it has."

Suddenly a sense of urgency gripped him, and he

161

heard Orl give a surprised rasping noise. A new memory unreeled in their minds, and Ross felt a familiar sinking sensation. The rate at which the energy drain on the computer's power center was increasing had suddenly speeded up. At the new rate, instead of another twenty hours of time in which to get their job done, they would be lucky to have ten!

The wall before them looked more solid and frustrating than ever.

CHAPTER 10

Kari looked puzzled. "Why won't the pistols work?"

"The wall includes a spell against them," Ross explained, rather pleased at having thought of an acceptable answer so rapidly.

"What about your magic hole diggers?" Kari asked. "The wall couldn't include a spell against them; nobody knew about them when it was built."

Ross blinked. Kari might have simplistic views on technology, but there was nothing wrong with her brain. The dynamite worked on an entirely different principle.

"I don't know," he said, "but we can try them. Do you still have the lighter?"

For answer, she pulled the four dynamite-laden arrows from her quiver, handed them to Ross, and then reached to the bottom of the quiver and came up with the lighter.

Ross gave three of the arrows back to her, and, borrowing her knife, cut the stick of dynamite from the other one. "You two get back down the tunnel," he said. "I'll light this and join you."

Kari looked as if she was going to object, but only for a moment. She was apparently still a bit subdued from her unfortunately timed rescue. As she and Orl trotted down the tunnel, Ross placed the dynamite against the approximate center of the door. As he reached down with the lighter, he wished there was some way of getting the explosive under the door; too much of the force was going to be wasted in the air this way. But the door fit the bottom of the tunnel so tightly that a knife-blade could not be forced between them.

He lit the end of the fuse and ran toward the fuzzy area of light that surrounded Orl and Kari a hundred yards or more down the tunnel. When he reached them, they all dropped to the floor, and a few seconds later the explosion jolted them. While it was more distant than the others had been, it seemed far louder in the enclosed space, and the echoes reverberated like receding artillery fire. As they lay waiting for silence to return, something struck the floor of the tunnel a few yards away. It wasn't large, but Ross winced at the thought of the tunnel roof giving way. Nothing else fell, however, and when silence returned they stood up and looked back toward the door. They could see nothing; the firefly glow of the light came nowhere near reaching the required distance.

Ross began trotting back toward the door. There had been no noises which might be construed as collapsing metal, so he was not surprised when he came close enough to see that the door still stood.

It was not totally undamaged, however. As he walked up to it, he could see a slight crack running up from the floor as far as the light extended. Ross pounded on the door on either side of the crack, but it seemed as solid as before.

At least it wasn't totally indestructable. He used two sticks of dynamite in his second attempt, wedging them tightly against the door and trying without much success to pack dirt around them. The blast set up a ringing in his eardrums that felt as though it was going to last a good long time, but it failed to budge the door. Several more cracks appeared, but even with all three of them pushing, the door refused to even bend slightly.

Ross looked at the last stick of dynamite dubiously. Judging from past attempts, it probably wouldn't weaken the door enough to let them through it, and the dynamite had been so useful so far that he hated to use up his last stick. Alternatives, however, seemed scarce. Other entrances to the transit system were all a long distance away, and all were farther from the computer section than the one they had used. And if this tunnel was blocked, there seemed no reason why others shouldn't be. Was the alien creature barricading itself? If it was, it would be unlikely to overlook any convenient access.

His memories showed him older entrances to the system, one of them very close to their destination—but those entrances had collapsed long ago and it would take a construction gang to open them again.

The connection was made instantaneously; construction gang—bulldozer! With this door presumably weakened considerably by the dynamite, he wouldn't need another entrance; the bulldozer should go right through it.

If they could get to the machine in time. . . .

His computer-induced memories told him they were less than a tenth of a day's travel from the Earth Gate. Kari, of course, could make it in half that time, but she would have very little luck in trying to operate the bulldozer.

With Ross in the lead, they hurried back to the last branch in the tunnel. Orl had no concept of what a bulldozer might be, but he seemed confident that Ross's predicted usefulness was finally showing. Kari accepted Ross's explanation that he needed some of the magic he had left at the Earth Gate.

Between the branch and the other entrance, there was only one place where the walls had partially collapsed, and the pile of rubble didn't look as if it would give too much trouble to the bulldozer. Ross hopefully quested through his memories for an alternative approach to the computer section through another set of tunnels, but came up with the same answer he had received before; conditions unknown and entrances too far away. If they couldn't break down that door, they weren't going to make it.

An hour or so later, the trio climbed the steps of the station, and Ross wondered about the bulldozer making it down those steps. But there was no point in wondering; it had to, and that was all there was to it. They hurried across the floor of the large room at the top of the stairs; Venntrans had evidently believed in making all their stations identical. A section of wall dilated for them, and as if in answer to Ross's unspoken question, it continued to expand until half the wall had vanished before shrinking to normal size. So they could get the bulldozer inside the station, at least.

If any other buildings had ever been near the station, they were long gone. Not even a piece of rubble was visible on the level grassland that surrounded it. A few charred tree trunks nearby bore testimony to the fire that had cleared the area, but even these were mouldering back into humus. Several hundred yards from the building, the forest resumed. In the entire clearing, nothing moved.

Even as Ross realized that he didn't know where the Earth Gate was from here, one of his new memories surfaced to show him. So, apparently, did one of Orl's, for they started off simultaneously. Kari, knowing only that they were guided by magic, followed them, keeping a

166

sharp watch in all directions. Once they were in the edge of the forest Ross felt more secure, though he knew the feeling was an illusion. The barbarians had found them easily enough in the forest before, and as for the thing that had taken over part of the computer, he had no idea of what its limitations, or even its intentions, were. There was no indication whether it knew where they were at any given time, or cared. Somehow, for some unknown reason, it had touched them briefly and departed. In the touching, it had very nearly driven them mad, as it had the Venntrans of long ago, but there was no way to tell whether their fear had produced joy, grief, indifference, or some other emotion in the thing, or whether it knew they had feared. Again, for no discernable reason, it had produced the animals.

But was there any reason to expect logical action from it? Certainly not human or Venntran logic. The creature—if it was a living being at all—was so different from them that common laws of nature seemed not to apply to it, so how could anything as arbitrary as human logic apply?

It acted according to its nature, the computer said, which was a nice phrase until one analyzed it. The thing's actions were determined by its nature—and observers could only determine its nature by its actions. So much for the all-knowing computer.

As if thinking about the creature had drawn its attention, Ross felt tendrils of irrational fear flick across his mind, and with it a moment of awareness. Even before he could react, it was gone, leaving him with an image of a vast formless body of—energy?—somehow imprisoned—in the computer section?—and frustrated in the accomplishment of some unfathomable task. With it were overtones of interest in emotions, though the nature of the interest was not clear. Scientific? Sadistic? A use for emotions; not as food, but as—a drug! For a moment everything seemed clear, and then Ross realized that he had only part of the answer. An addiction to emotions could explain a lot of things, such as Joe Kujawa's outburst when they had first entered Venntra, but it was blended with another, totally alien concept.

What was clear was that the being was definitely in the computer section. If it was attracted by emotion, then the approach of Ross, Orl and Kari would attract it, and bring down on them the same terror and madness they had felt during those brief touches.

They were going to have about as much chance of destroying it as the ancient Venntrans had.

The sun had gone down and a light rain was falling when they reached the Earth Gate. Ross went directly to where the bulldozer was hidden in the trees while Orl and Kari went into the Gate building to see if the food dispensers were working. On the bulldozer, Ross went through the seemingly endless steps necessary to start the starting motor and then get the diesel itself going and properly adjusted. Why, he wondered, couldn't a technology that sent men to the moon build a bulldozer that could be started with something less than fifty control and lever settings and a hundred different operator actions? When he finally had the diesel rumbling smoothly at the specified warmup rate, he jumped down and ran back to the Gate building, hoping that Orl had found things in operating condition.

The large door at the bottom of the ramp was open and Orl and Kari were waiting just inside, out of the rain. Kari pointed to the small room at one side and Ross collected a half dozen of the small food squares and gulped one down as he walked back to the outer door. The rest he tried to stuff into his pockets, only then discovering that the uniform had no pockets. Eventually he ate another of the squares and stuffed the rest into the pouch on top of the pistol, wondering if pockets were another thing unique to Earth. He avoided looking at the square in the center of the room and the rocks and dirt—from Earth!—scattered about the floor.

By the time they got back to the bulldozer, the warm-up period was completed and the monster was ready to move. Ross offered to let Kari squeeze into half of the cushioned but battered seat or perch on one of the broad, padded arms, but she preferred to walk. Even though she could see better from the bulldozer, she felt exposed, and she reacted to the rumbling of the machine with suspicion. Earth magic, compared to Venntran magic, was remarkably noisy. Ross also felt exposed and vulnerable but there was nothing he could do about it except wish that he had been driving one of the enclosed-cab models. Orl, though he was nervous about the exposure, decided that he couldn't keep up if he stayed on the ground. He half-sat on the right arm of the seat, and got as good a grip as he could on the handle which protruded from the fuel tank shell just behind the seat. It was precarious, but better than trying to keep up the six mile per hour pace on foot.

Ross handed his gun to Kari, who accepted it reluctantly and only after Ross explained that he couldn't drive and shoot both, and since all but one of the dynamite sticks were gone, her arrows weren't going to be as useful as a pistol.

As they rumbled out onto the road, Ross tried to remember how much fuel he had. Had he filled the machine that morning before he drove through the Gate, or had it been the night before? A tank holding 115 gallons sounded good, but it didn't take this monster long to use it up. He finally decided it didn't make a lot of difference; if they ran out, that was it, diesel fuel being in short supply on Venntra. The computer could probably produce any fuel required—after they had gone all the way back to the computer with a sample for analysis. The planet would be blowing up by that time. Anyway, he found it impossible to even make a good guess as to how much fuel would be needed to drive to the "infected" computer section and break down X number of doors along the way.

Whether the computer managed to divert any barbarian patrols, or the tremendous roar of the bulldozer engine made them keep their distance, or whether the barbarians just didn't like to go out in the rain, Ross was never sure. But none of the hissing little vehicles approached them during the time it took them to reach the transit system entrance. One of the bulldozer's front lights burned out, but there were no major problems with the machine. If it hadn't been for the rain and his worry about getting through the door when they arrived, Ross would have counted it one of his most pleasant experiences with a bulldozer, not that he had all that many pleasant memories of operating the machine to compare this one to. There wasn't even an animal stirring, and if there had been, he had difficulty imagining any animal that could have any effect on a bulldozer.

His imagination, however, was more versatile than he gave it credit for being. From somewhere in the dark, beyond the limit of the remaining three lights, there came a combination of bellow and scream that made the bulldozer's roar seem quiet. Orl jumped and almost fell off the seat. Kari, trotting along in the perimeter of the

170

light, stopped abruptly, her eyes darting in the direction of the sound. Ross, with the bulldozer already at top speed, could only keep it aimed directly ahead, into the clearing that surrounded the transit system entrance. Another minute or two was all they needed. If whatever it was would just hold off that long. . . .

It didn't. There was another scream, and something appeared at the edge of the area covered by the remaining front lamp. It advanced further into the light, its shaggy, tree-trunk legs pounding, its trunk swaying, its twisted tusks almost touching the ground.

You just had to think of animals, didn't you? a portion of Ross's mind sneered at him. *So now there's a mammoth between us and the transit building, and I hope you're satisfied.*

Out of the corner of his eye, Ross could see Orl fumbling for his pistol with one hand while he used the other to hang onto the bulldozer, and kept his eyes on the apparition ahead of them. Kari, her instinct overpowering her common sense, had already loosed an arrow at the beast. It smacked into the animal's shoulder with no more effect than a pinprick.

"Hang on!" Ross shouted to Orl. "I'm stopping!"

Afterwards, he decided that he'd have been better off to keep going, using the bulldozer's momentum to knock the beast out of the way. But at the time, all he thought about was the shock of impact. Even as he spoke, his hands were darting from lever to lever, releasing the flywheel clutch, reducing engine speed as it started to race with the load removed, slipping the gear stick into neutral, re-engaging the flywheel clutch, and muttering curses under his breath at the complexity of the operation. Before he had finished the operation, the machine ground to a halt, nearly throwing Orl onto one of the treads. As the mammoth bore down on them, still sounding like a ten-ton banshee, Ross raised the blade to meet it, and Orl clambered down to the ground.

"You're better off up here!" Ross yelled at him. "If that thing gets to you on the ground, all it has to do is step on you."

Orl waved his pistol. "I will be able to fire more effectively from the ground."

Before he could fire at all, there was a grinding crash as the tusks struck the raised blade, followed by a jar that shook Ross off his seat as the rest of the creature smashed into the machine, jolting it backwards several inches despite the locked threads.

Then the beast was backing away, rearing its trunk in the air, and Ross could see that one of its tusks was broken off about halfway down and there was a gaping wound in the forehead. No, not a wound; the mammoth was just as much a machine as the bulldozer. A break, then. It didn't seem to be inconvenienced by the damage. After surveying the opposition for a moment, it charged again.

Orl, in the meantime, had moved out so he could get a clear shot at the beast, and Kari had belatedly used her intelligence and exchanged her bow for the pistol, pointing it rather uncertainly at the mammoth.

A fiery beam shot from Orl's weapon, filling the night with sparkles as individual raindrops sparkled and vanished in its path. It hissed through the rain, and there was a loud crackling as it touched the mammoth's side and began to bore into it.

The mammoth continued its charge, veering toward the source of the beam. Kari's weapon came to life, catching the beast on the other side, beginning to eat a foot-wide hole into the gray, bloodless interior without even causing it to slow down.

"The legs!" Ross shouted. "Hit the legs!"

Almost simultaneously, the beams shifted like a pair of rocket trails through the rain-filled air. They focussed on the front legs as the beast thundered past the bulldozer and Orl dodged behind the machine. The mammoth took a swipe at him with its trunk as it passed and then swerved toward Kari, who was standing in the open, well away from any possible cover. Unable to do anything but watch, Ross sat helplessly as the beast seemed about to trample the girl into the ground. Then, only yards away, its front legs gave way and it tumbled forward, skidding to a stop so close that Kari could have reached out and touched it. The beams winked out.

But the artificial monster was not finished. The trumpeting, now so close as to be deafening, continued, and the trunk lashed out toward Kari, who leaped back out of the way. Even as Kari circled the monster and ran for the bulldozer, Ross could see the gouge in the thing's side beginning to fill in with the same greyish material that had been eaten away. The legs were beginning to reform as the stumps thrashed in the grass.

Ross watched for a moment in frozen fascination before turning to yell at his companions. "Get in the building!" he shouted. "I'll bring the bulldozer!"

Orl started a lumbering run across the clearing, while Kari followed him, pausing occasionally to check the whereabouts of the mammoth. Ross released the brake and managed to get the machine moving forward with only a couple of wasted motions. As the machine started rumbling forward, Ross squinted into the darkness beyond the headlamp's glow. Two or three hundred yards ahead he could see the faint luminescence that hovered

173

around the ghostly figures of Kari and Orl. Beyond them, the transit building showed faintly. Ross wished desperately that there was a way he could speed the bulldozer up, but short of getting off and pushing there was none. Behind him, at the edge of light from the rear lamps, he could see the mammoth beginning to struggle to its feet. How was it doing it? Ross knew that the computer—and thus the alien thing infecting one of its sections—was capable of creating artificial animals or almost anything else. But out of thin air, on the spot?

Another memory. The transit system had been abandoned when the computer superseded the distribution system with a program of creating whatever the Venntrans desired, in their own homes. Had the alien being extended the process a step further?

Ross darted a look ahead to see how far he had to go. Too far, at this speed; the mammoth was starting after him.

Abruptly he put the brakes to one tread and the machine spun around until it faced the mammoth. At the same time he slammed the direction lever into reverse, so that by the time the turn was completed and the brake released, the machine was moving at full speed in reverse, which amounted to a whole seven miles an hour. The increase in speed wasn't all that thrilling, but the maneuver had put the bulldozer blade between Ross and the mammoth and his shoulders could quit prickling from the anticipation of having a trunk wrapped around them from behind.

Keeping his hands on the steering clutch levers, he twisted in the seat so he could see where he was going. Still a good distance away, the entrance had dilated enough for Orl and Kari to get inside, but was still a long way from big enough for the bulldozer. Ross wondered what would happen if he tried to go through it before it was quite wide enough, and decided he didn't want to find out. He tried to aim more directly at the opening, but, as he almost always did when backing up, he used the wrong clutch and found himself veering the wrong way. With a growing feeling of panic, he shoved at the other lever and the machine swung back, but overshot.

Then he heard the trumpeting scream of the mammoth again, and it sounded closer. Or was it his imagination? *The whole blasted creature is my imagination!* he thought. *Why can't I unimagine it?* Having the bulldozer blade as protection was good, but he wished he could see what the mammoth was doing. Then it loomed up almost on top of him and watching what it was doing didn't seem like such a good idea, particularly if what it was doing was pulling him off the bulldozer and trampling him into jelly. Its legs seemed as good as new—which they were, he realized. He wondered if he should dive off the machine and run for it. If the animal would attack the bulldozer instead of him. . . .

A column of sparking, hissing fire lanced past Ross, and the mammoth's forehead erupted in crackling disintegration. The artificial monster lurched into the side of the bulldozer while Ross frantically hung on to whatever levers he could reach, and then sprawled thunderously to the ground.

The door of the building, now only yards away, swelled outward raggedly, its edges fuzzy and indistinct, trembling as if it was an effort to hold that much dilation. With a final maneuver of the steering clutch levers Ross was through the opening, and almost before the machine had cleared it, the opening seemed to collapse upon itself and the wall was blank and solid.

Ross brought the machine to a stop and let out his breath in a huge, lung-emptying sigh. He was trembling all over. He sat there for several seconds, breathing deeply and getting his nerves settled. Orl and Kari came over and looked at him expectantly. Ross blinked at them and then pulled himself erect in the seat. The trembling gradually faded away, leaving only the vibration from the engine.

"Okay," Ross said, turning the bulldozer around and starting for the stairway, "the easy part is over. Now for the real problems."

CHAPTER 11

Getting the bulldozer down the steps was less trouble than Ross expected. There was a moment of nervousness and vertigo as the huge machine rocked at the top of the stairs and finally tilted forward, but the slope was less than 45 degrees and the treads caught on the edges of the seemingly indestructable steps and kept the bulldozer from sliding all the way to the bottom. His only problem was to keep the brakes applied equally to both treads; otherwise the machine had a tendency to go down sideways instead of nose first.

Once at the bottom, they moved along at the top speed except when negotiating obstacles. Orl remained on the arm of the bulldozer seat, hanging on grimly, while Kari trotted along side. Ross marveled at her endurance.

In little more than half an hour they reached the door that blocked their way. Orl and Kari both stood well back at Ross's insistence, and he wished once again that he had been driving an enclosed cab model. If any part of this door decided to fall back on top of him, he was going to be in big trouble.

Deciding to start as easily as possible, he nosed the machine up to the door until the blade was touching it. Then, in low gear, he tried to move forward. Nothing happened except for the treads skidding on the tunnel floor.

He backed up a few feet and came forward, still in low gear, at little more than two miles per hour. Even at that speed, the blade crashed into the door with a resounding thud. The door seemed to sway a trifle, but held firm. There wasn't even another crack in it to show for the effort.

All right, Ross thought. *All or nothing. Full speed ahead, and damn the obstructions. I regret that I have but one life to give for my computer. Win one for the Gipper.* He backed away a good distance, put the machine into high gear, and thundered forward. Even at the modest top speed of which the machine was capable, roughly eighteen tons of bulldozer generated a lot of force. The bottom of the blade, which struck first, snapped off, the struts and hydraulic linkages that controlled the blade bent and ruptured, and the remaining front headlight disintegrated.

In the midst of the noise of tearing metal and the roaring engine, there was a sound like a thousand panes of glass shattering. A network of tiny cracks appeared in the door. For a moment there was no motion, and then a section of door thirty feet high and nearly as wide simply collapsed, falling away from the machine.

Ross backed up, turning the bulldozer so the rear lights pointed at the opening. The collapsed portion of the door was a pile of dust with a few larger chunks of material mixed with it. Getting down to examine it, Ross saw that it was apparently similar to the material that lined the tunnel walls, except that it was not transparent and was considerably thicker, the overall thickness being at least a quarter of an inch. Beyond the opening, the tunnel stretched, empty.

As Ross backed the bulldozer through the opening a few seconds later, he noticed that the remains of the blade dragged on the floor, adding a scraping as of a giant fingernail on a super-blackboard to the engine roar. He tried to lift it, but aside from a brief twitch, nothing happened. He decided he was lucky that the machine was still operable; the blade and its linkages had presumably taken most of the shock.

Then he noticed the skeletons lying in a corner formed by the door and the tunnel wall. A small group of them lay there, pressed against the door as if their last actions had been to try to force themselves through it. All wore the black uniforms of the barbarians, the same that Ross was now wearing. Or more or less wearing, considering the missing sleeves and various holes and rips in the material. Next to two of the skeletons lay pistols, and there was evidence of a violent conclusion to whatever affair had taken place here. About the necks of all were tiny medallions, and the sight of these brought another memory to the fore of Ross's mind. Many years ago when the barbarians first discovered the computer, it had tried sending a party of them through these tunnels to the infected section of itself. None had returned, and The House Which Is Not Entered had been given its name. Ross felt a chill, and glanced apprehensively down the tunnel. A line from *Treasure Island* forced its unwanted way into his thoughts; "Six they were, and six are we; and bones is what they are now." Except there were only three in this group. The barbarians had failed; was there any reason to believe this attempt would be more successful?

We're more advanced, he told himself firmly, and another part of his mind said, *Sure, that's why Kari keeps pulling you out of trouble.*

No point in sitting here and worrying, though. "Let's go," he said. "Who wants a ride?"

Orl climbed over the tread and onto the arm of the seat and resumed his grip on the handle behind the seat. Kari was still looking nervously at the skeletons. Ross should, he felt, try to explain this last bit of information, but. . . .

The medallions! If they were still working, the computer could do its own explaining. He kicked on the brake lock and climbed down. "More magic", he told Kari as he squatted next to one of the skeletons and removed the medallion. "For you, this time, if the magic is still working."

She looked at him oddly. "I am not a magician," she said a bit defiantly, "but everything has been magic today."

Ross dusted off the medallion and saw that its center showed the same star-flecked blackness that his own displayed at times. He hoped that meant it was still working. He handed it to Kari.

"Put this around your neck," he said. "It will make thoughts appear in your mind, just as this," pointing to his own medallion, "makes thoughts appear in mine."

"True thoughts?" Kari inquired as she hesitantly took the medallion, and then before Ross could answer she slipped it over her head, twitching slightly as the grey chain shifted and settled into place.

A moment later her eyes widened, and Ross wondered how much the computer was telling her, and in what terms her own mind was receiving the information. After several moments of silence, a frown appeared on her face. "Why are we standing here?" she asked sharply. "We must not waste time!"

She began moving down the tunnel, and Ross hurriedly climbed aboard the bulldozer and started after her. With both front headlights gone, this required backing the machine, and twisting in the seat to see where he was going.

They had gone perhaps a mile beyond the door, and Ross's neck was beginning to ache from the unaccustomed position, when he felt the first touch of fear. Somewhere ahead the being lay waiting for them, and the image of a huge, coiled snake flickered through his mind.

He jerked involuntarily on the controls and tried to drive the thought from his mind. Another memory appeared, attempting to reassure him. The ability to create artificial animals or anything else was somehow tied to computer "perceptors" which were placed to cover the surface of Venntra but had never been installed in the tunnels, there being no need for them there. Any animals down here would be purely imaginary, not the three-dimensional reproductions that had appeared on the surface.

The information should have calmed Ross, but it didn't. He could still see the snake, and now it was slithering along the ground somewhere above his head. Even if it existed in reality and not his imagination it couldn't get at him here, but that knowledge failed to help. The knowledge was logical and rational, and the fear was not.

"It is beginning," Orl's rasping voice said, almost in Ross's ear.

"You can feel it too, then?" Ross asked, forcing his voice to be calm.

"It is very much as it was before," Orl answered. The fingers of his free hand were flexing in a continuous but uneven motion. "I believe," the saurian continued after a moment's silence, "that I shall be able to control my reactions, now that I am aware of the cause."

"I hope so," Ross said, but he wondered. A billion Venntrans had perished in fear and madness; what

181

chance did this one remote descendent of theirs have? And if Orl failed, how could Ross and Kari see the controls and find the right ones to disconnect?

For another quarter of a mile, the fear built higher and higher, toward sheer terror. At first the roaring diesel had helped to blot out the thoughts of what lay ahead, but now it was merely background noise. The blackness beyond the lights was filled with a thousand nebulous, uncertain creatures, creatures against which the computer could not protect him because the computer understood them no better than he did. Telling himself they didn't exist except in his imagination failed to convince the atavistic part of his mind that believed in ghoulies and ghosties. He began to shiver, and his hands shook on the controls.

Suddenly Kari stopped in front of the machine. She stood as rigid as a statue, and Ross could see that her mouth was tightly clenched. The medallion was gone from around her neck. He stopped the bulldozer barely in time to keep from running over her.

Without warning, Orl leaped from his seat. As he stepped on the tread, which was still moving slowly, his foot twisted and he sprawled to the ground. Before Ross could start to climb down, Orl had scrambled up and began limping rapidly back the way they had come. As if released from a trance, Kari dropped her bow and raced after him. Ross climbed stiffly down from the machine and took up the chase, and as he ran, some small measure of control returned. It was as if, by sheer physical exertion, he could partially fight off the effects of the creature.

Kari caught Orl within a few yards and clamped a hand on his shoulder, dug in her heels and pulled him off balance. He swung an arm back as if to strike her,

182

but stopped before the swing was completed. He stood rigidly for a moment, his eyes looking straight ahead.

"I now have myself under control, I believe," Orl's voice rasped at them. "But I feel it would be safer if we abandoned our Venntran weapons. I no longer trust myself with mine."

He slowly took the pistol from its pouch, turned to face the direction they had come, and hurled the gun as far as he could. Ross took his own pistol, which Kari had returned to him once they reached the transit building, and looked at it. They might well need it before they were done—but he recalled the skeletons back at the door. The barbarians hadn't removed their weapons, and by the look of things, had died by them. Reluctantly, he tossed the gun away. As it vanished into the darkness, he had difficulty in keeping himself from running after it.

Stiffly, their attention concentrated on making their own muscles obey them, they walked back to the bulldozer.

We can't take much more, Ross thought. *How much farther is it?*

The answer floated up to him. Far down the tunnel there was a dim light, the same firefly glow that hovered about the wearers of the medallions.

A surge of hope shot through Ross, but it was brief. As they came up to the bulldozer, a snarling whimper came from Orl's lipless mouth. The saurian took another step, slowly, stiffly, like someone in a dream. He began another step, his foot lifting slowly from the floor of the tunnel, and stopped. His entire leg began to tremble; then his body began shaking. His eyes glazed and, a moment later, rolled upward. Slowly, a muscle at a time, the saurian's body relaxed and collapsed to the floor.

Ross knelt beside Orl, took his shoulders and shook them. The head wobbled limply. Except for the breathing, he could have been dead. Ross let him fall back to the floor. They had no way to rouse him, and no assurance that rousing him would do any good. The only one of the trio who could read the controls of the safeguards had been the first to fall. What could they do now?

A glance at his watch told Ross that they still had a few hours to go. They could take Orl back down the tunnel, where he might revive. Perhaps he could describe the control layout. If the barbarians could operate invisible controls on the cars, maybe Ross could memorize a few in a power supply. At least, farther away from this continuous barrage of terror they could think clearly.

Then from nowhere a thought appeared in Ross's mind, and he knew they had no time to retreat. They didn't have hours; they had minutes. In the last few minutes, as they had forced themselves forward against the driving fear, the alien creature's energy consumption had shot up again.

"Why?" Ross screamed into the medallion as though it was a radio transmitter.

"That it its nature," came the thought in reply.

Unable to accept such an answer, Ross's mind continued to whirl. Was their own proximity to the creature causing the trouble? Was this thing, whatever it was, experiencing something similar to what they were experiencing? Was it driven into terror and madness by their very nearness, and trying to protect itself by striking out blindly at a universe that it understood no better than the universe understood it? Striking out, drawing on the only source of power it had available; the computer power center.

Whatever the reason, the result would be the same. In a very few minutes the central power system was going to overload and turn Venntra into a collection of asteroids.

Ross stood up and looked at the bulldozer. It was powerful, but he didn't need power now, and if the terror built up any more he wouldn't be able to handle the controls. Physical exertion had helped before, so the best idea would be to run for that mocking little glow ahead.

And if he got there, what would he do then?

Kari leaned down stiffly to pick up her bow, and Ross saw the arrows in her quiver.

An idea surged to the surface of his mind. "The dynamite—the magic hole digger," he said. "Give it to me. And the lighter."

Carefully controlling her movements, Kari took the arrow with the dynamite from her quiver and handed it to him. Not trusting himself to unfasten it from the arrow, he held arrow and all while Kari produced the lighter, and handed it to him.

"I can help," she said.

"There's nothing you can do. Get on back down the tunnel where the fear is less."

"You can destroy this thing?"

"Maybe, if I can get to it."

"I will come with you," she said. "I will help."

He looked at her. She was keeping a rigid control over her body, but her face showed more terror than he felt.

"All right," he said. He reached down and took the medallion from Orl's neck. "Put this on and keep it on. If I don't make it all the way, try to keep going. This

185

magic disc will tell you where to put the magic stick. Place it there, light it, and get away."

"I will try."

"We'll have a better chance if we run."

They walked back a few steps. In just those few feet, Ross could feel the lessening of the fear, and he had an almost overwhelming desire to keep going, regardless of consequences. If he was going to fail anyway, why shouldn't he spend his last minutes in relative comfort?

But there was still a chance. He was on his feet, still able to think, and the goal was in sight. One last dash might do it.

"As fast as you can," he said. "Drag me if I slow down. Now!"

Together they started forward at a run, their feet pounding on the barren tunnel floor. For the first few yards, while they were still within range of the bulldozer's lights, their progress seemed to get easier as the physical strain of running took some of the chill from their bodies and some of the cloud of horror from their minds.

Then it began to build again. Going into the darkness with only the diffuse glow of their madallions to see by was like plunging into a gradually thickening wall of water. Ross wondered if it wouldn't have been better to go in on the bulldozer, with its lights dispelling some of the fears, but it was too late for that now.

Ahead was blackness, and in that blackness, Ross knew, waited all the horrors that Earth and Venntra could suply. A coiled snake hissed and struck, there in the darkness. He could feel its venom as it sprayed toward him, feel the cold, slimy skin as it slid over him. His rational objection that snakes aren't slimy did noth-

186

ing to dispell the illusion; he could feel a repulsive trail of ichor across his skin. A monstrous spider leaped through the blackness, and he felt its bulbous, pulsing body over his face, its spindly, hairy legs writhing about his head as it struggled to keep a grip on him. He was wading through giant leeches, while rats swarmed at his legs and maggots worked in his flesh. He opened his mouth to scream, and he felt the spider's furry belly scrape against his tongue, fill his mouth, and muffle the cry.

Suddenly, he could feel his mind split. One second he was struggling through the blackness of the tunnel floor, besieged by every fear that his subconscious mind could produce. The next second he was watching himself from a distance. It was similar to his reaction to the visions of the ancient Venntrans. Somehow, the rational observer had separated from the part of him that lived through the horrors.

It wasn't even himself down there on the tunnel floor, the detached part of his mind showed him; it was not Ross Allen. Instead, his mind with its own brand of insane logic, produced Commander Freff. Every blond hair in place, steely eyes glinting with determination, the lithe muscular form, as always, fit for action, the Commander was not to be daunted by a few monsters. He clawed the gigantic spider from his face and hurled it against the far wall of the tunnel. Lashing out with a deadly accuracy, he smashed the head of the snake even as it struck. His polished boots spurned the rat hordes underfoot. Commander Freff, the magical creation of Ross's mind, battered his way through the magical creations of the alien and into the dim light beyond.

As Ross and the Commander ran forward, Ross saw Kari stiffen and fall. Her legs would no longer carry

187

her into the weight of terror opposing them, but she looked up at Ross as he ran past and crawled a few more feet before her terror left her unconscious.

Ross and the Commander entered the dimly lighted area which was the computer section. Nightmarish creatures crawled and flopped, obscuring the machinery in the room. But somehow, Ross knew where to place the charge, and he directed the Commander's fingers as they forced the arrowhead into a crevice between two panels and lit the fuse.

Then Ross was free to give way to the horrors of his mind and stagger back down the tunnel. Somehow, he forced himself to stop by Kari's body, and with a strength he didn't know he possessed, he picked her up and stumbled on into the blackness.

He was still struggling down the tunnel when the explosion came, knocking him to the floor and rolling both he and Kari several feet along the tunnel. As they lay there, stunned by the explosion and still mentally retreating from the terror around them, there was another sound. First it was a crackling, the kind Ross remembered hearing once when a downed high voltage line had welded itself to a metal fence. Then there was a keening, banshee wail, and a rattle of small explosions like machine-gun fire. Finally, the wail died away into silence.

Then, there was peace. The alien being was gone.

It was several hours later before they felt like attempting the walk back down the tunnel. The bulldozer had stopped; whether it had run out of fuel or had been damaged in the final explosion Ross didn't know and didn't feel like inspecting to find out. Maybe he'd come back and look at it later; for now, farewell thou good and faithful steed.

As they walked, they conferred with the computer.

"It is now possible to reopen the Gates," the computer informed them. You may return to Elsprag, to Earth, and to Leean, if you desire."

"Not to Leean," Kari said. "I have become too used to magic since coming here, and there was never anything on Leean I cared about."

Ross's first reaction was elation. He'd won the battle, and now he could take his reward and go home and relax. The Commander Freff adventures could get off to a rousing beginning, with the material he'd learned here. "The Intergalactic Infection" would be a lovely title.

My duty is to reopen the Gate and inform the scientists of Elsprag that we are no longer cut off," Orl said. "After that . . . well, perhaps I can return with the scientific team. After all, I am the expert on the planet now; I believe I can convince them that they need me."

"You aren't going to stay on Elsprag?" Ross asked, surprised. "I thought you'd have had enough of imagination and illogic by now."

Orl rotated his head negatively. "This imagination of yours appears to be a powerful force. It would be interesting to study it."

"It can be pretty dangerous when it isn't controlled," Ross said.

"Then we will have to learn to control it," Orl answered.

"If you get the chance," Kari said. "You haven't said what you would do, Rossallen. If you go back to Earth, there won't be any imagination here for Orl to study."

Listening to Orl, Ross had begun having second thoughts. "If I do return to Earth," he asked the computer, "is there any possibility that a Gate will be built so that I can return here?"

"The probability is small," the computer told him.

"To build a Gate from Earth to Venntra, Elspragan scientists would have to go through the Gate to Earth together with the materials required for its construction. There is much for them to do here; it does not seem probable that time can be spared for such a venture."

Not to mention what would happen to them when they stepped through to Earth, Ross thought. So if he went back, it would be a one-way trip. He looked at Kari.

"Come to think of it," he said, "you haven't said what you're going to do. All you said was that you didn't want to go back to Leean."

Kari looked uncomfortable. "Is it necessary for me to decide now?" she asked irritably.

Ross made his decision. "Yes, because what you decide is going to affect what I do. If I stay here, will you stay with me?"

Suddenly she was smiling at him. "I couldn't decide because I didn't know what you were going to do. If you are going to be here, then I will be here."

"And when I get back from Elsprag," Orl said, we can study the Venntran civilization—and magic—together."

But Ross and Kari were too absorbed in one another's magic to hear him.

free!

Important Questionnaire

We value your opinion. Please give us your reactions to **Gates of the Universe** in order to help us make this new series of LASER Books the very best in exciting reading entertainment. Your FREE BOOK, **Seeds of Change**, will be sent to you immediately upon receipt of this completed questionnaire. (Please check (✓) the appropriate boxes.)

1. What prompted you to buy **Gates of the Universe**?
   ☐ Cover Design ☐ Story Outline ☐ Price

2. Did you enjoy this LASER Book?
   ☐ Yes   ☐ No

3. Were you sufficiently pleased to purchase other LASER Books?
   ☐ Yes   ·   ☐ No

4. What type of stories do you generally read?
   ☐ Sci. Fiction ☐ Mystery & Suspense
   ☐ Westerns   ☐ Adventure
   ☐ Other (please specify)

5. At what store did you purchase this novel?
   ☐ Book   ☐ Cigar   ☐ Supermkt.
   ☐ Drug   ☐ Department   ☐ Chain

6. Please indicate your general age group.
   ☐ Under 20 yrs. ☐ 30 - 50 yrs.
   ☐ 20 - 30 yrs. ☐ Over 50 yrs.

For your **FREE LASER BOOK**, MAIL YOUR COMPLETED QUESTIONNAIRE TO:

Seeds of Change
LASER READER SERVICE
M.P.O. Box 788, Niagara Falls, N.Y. 14302

*Cdn. Residents: Send to Stratford, Ont., Canada

Name . . . .
Address. . . . .
City/Town . . . ., ...
State/Prov. . . . . Zip/Postal Code . . . .